DOCTOR WHO
THE MYTH MAKERS

Based on the BBC television serial by Donald Cotton by arrangement with the British Broadcasting Corporation

DONALD COTTON

**Number 97
in the
Doctor Who Library**

A TARGET BOOK
published by
the Paperback Division of
W.H. ALLEN & Co. PLC

A Target Book
Published in 1985
By the Paperback Division of
W.H. Allen & Co. PLC
44 Hill Street, London W1X 8LB

First published in Great Britain by
W.H. Allen & Co. PLC in 1985

Printed and bound in Great Britain by
Anchor Brendon Ltd, Tiptree, Essex

The BBC producer of *The Myth Makers*
was John Wiles,
the director was Michael Leeston-Smith.

ISBN 0 426 20170 1

**To Humphrey Searle,
who wrote the music**

CONTENTS

1

Homer Remembers

Look over here; here, under the olive-trees – that's right, by the pile of broken stones and the cracked statues of old gods. What do you see?

Why, nothing but an old man, sitting in the Autumn sunshine; and dreaming; and remembering. That is what old men do, having nothing better to occupy their time... and since that is what I have become, that is why I do it.

I heard your footsteps when you first entered the grove; so sit down, whoever you are and have a slice of goat's cheese with me. There – it's rather good, you'll find; I eat very little else these days. Teeth gone, of course...

You think it's sad to be old? Nonsense – it's a triumph! An unexpected one, at that; because, I tell you, I never thought I'd make it past thirty! Men do not frequently survive to senility in these dangerous times. But then, being blind, I suppose I can hardly be considered much of a threat to anyone; so somehow I have been allowed to live... although probably more by negligence than by charity, or a proper concern for the elderly.

And I am grateful; for I have a tale or two still to tell, and a song or two to compose and throw to posterity... before I pass Acheron, and meet my dead friends in the shadows of the nether world.

I am, you see, a myth maker; and my name is Homer. I don't know if that will mean anything to you. But it is a name once well considered in poetic circles. No matter... no reputation lasts forever.

But that is why I sit here, in the stubble of the empty fields, and lean against the rubble of the fallen city which once was Troy; while the scavengers flap in the ruins, and the lizards run across my bare feet – at least, I hope they're lizards! If they are scorpions, perhaps you would be so kind? Thank you! And I remember the beginning of it all, long ago when I was young. Listen...

I was a wanderer then, as I am now – and so thoroughly undistinguished in appearance that I could pass unnoticed when men of greater consequence would, at the very least, be asked to give an account of themselves. But I was not blind in those days; and though I could do little to influence, I could at least observe the course of events; and to some extent – not being a complete fool – interpret them.

And what events they were! Troy – this mound of masonry behind us – was then the greatest city in the world. Although I must admit, that wasn't too difficult a trick, because the world then was not as it is known to be now.

A rather small flat disc, it was considered to be; and the latest geographical thinking was that it balanced rather precariously on the back of an elephant, which, for some reason, was standing on a tortoise! All nonsense, of course; we know now that the disc is very much larger and floats on some kind of metaphysical river; although I must say, I don't quite follow the argument myself.

At all events, it was bounded to the East by the Ural Mountains, where the barbarians lived; and to the West, just beyond the Pillars of Hercules, it fell away to night and old chaos. And what happened to the North and South we didn't like to enquire. All we were absolutely sure of was that the available space was a bit on the cramped side.

And the Trojans appeared to have rather more than their fair share of it. In fact, they sat four-square on most of

10

Asia Minor; and that, as I need hardly remind you, meant that they controlled the trade-routes through the Bosphorus. Which left my fellow-countrymen, the Greeks, with no elbow room at all to speak of; and they were, very naturally, mad as minotaurs about the whole situation.

Agamemnon, King of Mycenae, was their war-leader; but the trouble was he couldn't think of any excuse for starting a war, and that made things difficult for him. Men always need a cause before they embark on conquest, as is well known. Often it is some trifling difference of philosophy or religion; sometimes the revival of an ancient boundary dispute, the origins of which have long been forgotten by all sensible people. But no – in spite of sitting up nights and going through the old documents, and spending days bullying the historians, Agamemnon just couldn't seem to find one.

And then, just as it was beginning to look as if he'd have to let the whole thing slide, the Trojans themselves handed it to him on a platter! Well, one Trojan did, actually; and it was a beauty – adultery!

The adulterer in question was Paris, second son of Priam, King of Troy. Perhaps you will have heard of *La Vie Parisienne*. Well then, I need hardly say more: except perhaps, in mitigation, that the second sons of Royal Houses – especially if they are handsome as the devil – have a lot of temptation to cope with. And then, the unlikelihood of their ever achieving the throne does seem to induce irresponsibility which – combined, of course, with an inflated income – how shall I put it? – well, it aggravates any amorous propensities they may have. And, by Zeus, Paris had them! In overabundance and to actionable excess! He was – not to put too fine a point upon it – both a spendthrift and a lecher. He also had the fiendishly dangerous quality of charm: a bad combination, as you'll agree.

Well, we all know about princes and their libidinous ways: their little frolics below stairs – their engaging stage-door haunting jaunting? Just so. And if we are charitable, we turn a blind eye. But apparently, this sort of permissible regal intrigue wasn't enough for Paris. Listen – he first of all seduced, and then – Heaven help us all! – *abducted* the *Queen* of Sparta! Yes, I thought you'd sit up!

Her name was Helen and she was the wife of his old friend Menelaus. And Menelaus – wait for it – just happened to be Agamemnon's younger brother! So there you are!

Leaning over backwards to find excuses for Paris, I suppose one should admit that Helen *was* the most beautiful woman in the world. Or so people said; although how one can possibly know without conducting the most exhausting research, I cannot imagine. Possibly, Paris had – but even so! And then, having abducted her, to bring her home to meet his parents! The mind reels!

Anyway – while Menelaus himself was pardonably upset, his big brother, Agamemnon, was secretly delighted! Just the thing he'd been waiting for! Summoning a hasty conference of kings, at which he boiled with well-simulated apoplectic fury – the Honour of Greece at stake, et cetera – he roused their indignation to the pitch of a battle fleet; and they set sail for Troy on a just wave of retribution.

But if Agamemnon had done his homework properly, he'd have known that Troy was a very tough nut to crack – by no means the little mud-walled city-state he was used to. Impregnable is the word – although you might not think it now. And the Greeks seemed to have left their nut-crackers at home.

So for ten long years – if you believe me – the Greek Heroes sat outside those enormous walls, quarrelling amongst themselves and feeling rather silly; while any virtuous anger they may once have felt evaporated in the heat of home-thoughts and of the girls they'd left behind them.

And this was the stalemate situation when some trifling, forgotten business of a literary nature first brought me to the Plain of Scamander, where Troy's topless towers sat like the very symbol of permanence, and the Greek camp faded and festered in the summer haze.

Well, it had been a long journey: and, since nobody seemed to mind, I lay down on the river bank and went to sleep.

2

Zeus Ex Machina

Two men were fighting in a field, and the sound of it woke
me. The noise was excessive! There was, of course, the
clash of sword on armour, and mace on helm – you will
have read about such things – and these I might have
tolerated, merely pulling my cloak over my head with a
muttered groan, or a stifled sigh – it matters little which.

But, for some reason, they had chosen to accompany
their combat with an ear-splitting stream of bellowed
imprecations and rhetorical insult, the like of which I had
seldom heard outside that theatre – what's its name? – in
Athens. You know the one: big place – all right if it isn't
raining, and if you care for such things. Which I must say,
I rather do! But not, thank you, in the middle of a summer
siesta, on a baking hot Asiatic afternoon, when my feet
hurt and my head aches! The dust, too – they were kicking
up clouds of it, as they snarled and capered and gyrated!
Made me sneeze...

'In another moment,' I thought, 'somone will get hurt –
and I hope it isn't me.'

Because they don't care, these sort of people, who they
involve, once they get going. Blind anger, I think it's
called. So I got up cautiously, well-hidden behind a clump
of papyrus, or something – you can be sure of that. And
having nothing to do and being thoroughly awake now –
damn it! – I watched and listened, as is my professional
habit...

They were both big men; but one was enormous with

14

muscles queuing up behind each other, begging to be given a chance. This whole, boiling-over physique was restrained, somewhat inadequately, by bronze-studded, sweat-stained leather armour, which, no doubt, smelled abominable, and which creaked and groaned with his every action-packed movement. One could hardly blame it! To confine, even partially, such bursting physical extravagance, was – the leather probably felt – far beyond the call of duty, or of what the tanners had led it to expect.

Seams stretched and gussets gaped. On his head was a towering, beplumed horse's head helmet, which he wore as casually as if it were a shepherd's sheepskin cap: and this, of course, meant that he was a horse-worshipping Trojan, not a Greek. Furthermore, in view of everything else about him, he could only be the renowned Hector, King Priam's eldest son, and war-lord of Troy.

His opponent was a different matter; younger by some ten years, I would say, and with the grace of a dancer. Which he certainly needed, as he spun and pirouetted to avoid the great bronze, two-handed sword which Hector wielded – in *one* hand – as casually as though it was a carving knife in the hands of a demented chef.

He was more lightly armoured than Hector: but I couldn't help feeling that this was not so much a matter of military requirement, as of pride in the displaying of his perfectly proportioned body. He had that look of Narcissistic petulance one so often sees on the faces of health fanatics, or on male models who pose for morally suspect sculptors. I believe the Greeks have a word for it nowadays.

So, although I felt a certain sympathy for him at being so obviously out of his league, I must confess I didn't like him. I wondered who he could be. Hector was so notoriously invincible, that during the course of this ridiculous war he had been avoided by the Greeks as scrupulously as tax-inspectors are shunned by writers. Even the mighty Ajax, I had heard, had pleaded a migraine on being invited to indulge in single combat with him; and yet here was this slender, skipping, ballet-boy, obviously intent on pursuing the matter to the foregone conclusion of his being sliced into more easily disposable sections, and fed to the jackals. Who, I may say, were even now circling the improvized arena with an eye to business.

But the question of his identity was soon solved, as the two heroes paused for a gulp of dust...

'Out of breath so soon, Achilles, my lightfoot princeling?' inquired the giant politely. 'Your friend, Patroclus fled me further, and made better sport.'

So there I had it. Achilles and Patroclus: their relationship was well-known – and it explained everything.

'Murderer!', spat Achilles, without wit, 'Patroclus was a boy.' A boy? Quite so. To understand is not necessarily to approve.

'A boy, you say?' said Hector warming to his theme: 'Well he died most like a dog, whimpering for his master. Did you not hear him? He feared the dark, and was loth to enter it without you! Come – let me send you to him, where he waits in Hades! Let me throw him a bone or two!'

Well, what *can* you say to a remark like that? But after a moment's thought Achilles achieved the following:

'Your bones would be the meatier, Trojan, though meat a trifle run to fat. Well all's one... they will whiten
    well enough in the sun –
They may foul the air a little, but the world will be the
    sweeter for it.'

Not bad, really, on the spur of the moment: especially if you have to speak in that approximation to blank verse, which for some reason, heroes always adopt at times like these. (We shall notice the phenomenon again and it is as well to be prepared.)

But Hector was not to be discouraged by such rudimentary rodomantade, and chose to ignore it.

'Run, Achilles, run! Run just a little more, before you die! What, don't you *want* to leave a legend? Wouldn't you

16

like the poets to sing of you, eh? Not even to be the swiftest of the Greeks? Must I rob you of even that small distinction?'

Achilles was noticably piqued... after all he'd won prizes... 'Hector, by all the gods, I swear...' he said, and subsided, speechless.

Hector knew he'd made a good debating point, and sneered triumphantly. 'The gods? What gods? Do you dare to swear by *your* petty pantheology? That ragbag of squabbling, hobble-de-hoy Olympians – those little gods to frighten children? What sort of gods are those for a man to worship?'

And now, by a curious coincidence, there came a rumble of thunder, as one of those summer storms that pester the Aegean came flickering up from the South ... and Achilles could take a cue when he heard one...

'Beware the voice of Zeus, Hector! Beware the rage of Olympus!' The remark didn't go down at all well.

'Ha! Who am I to fear the thunder, you superstitious, dart-dodging decadent? Hear me, Zeus: accept from me the life of your craven servant, Achilles! Or else, I challenge you: descend to earth and save him.'

And, at that moment, the most extraordinary thing happened: even now, I can hardly believe my memory, or find words to describe it. But I swear there came a noise reminiscent of a camel in the last stages of dementia praecox; and, out of nowhere, there appeared on the plains beside us a small dark blue building of indeterminate architecture! It was certainly nothing of Greek or Asiatic origin; it was like nothing I had ever seen in all my travels; and, as I know now, it was the TARDIS...!

3

Hector Forgets

You, of course, whoever you are, will probably have heard of the TARDIS. There has certainly been enough talk about it since! At the time, however, I had not, and you may well imagine the effect that its sudden appearance produced – not only upon my apprehensive self – but upon the two posturing fighting-cocks before me. To say we were all flabbergasted is scarcely adequate... but perhaps it will serve for the moment?

Mind you, we Greeks are constantly expecting the materialisation of some god or other, agog to intervene in human affairs. Well, no – to be honest – not really *expecting*. Put it this way, our religious education has prepared us to accept it, *should* it occur. But that is by no means to say we anticipate it as a common phenomenon. It's the sort of thing that happens to *other* people, perhaps; but hardly before one's own eyes in the middle of everyday affairs, such as the present formalistic blood-letting. Certainly not. No – but, as I say, the church has warned us of the possibility, however remote.

The Trojans, on the other hand, as you will have gathered from Hector's nihilistic comments, have no such uncomfortable superstitions to support them in their hour of need.

Oh, they will read entrails with the best of them, and try to probe the future as one does; but as far as basic theology is concerned, they begin and end with the horse. That surprises you? Well, it's not a bad idea, when you think about it: after all, it was their cavalry that put them where they are today... or rather where they were yesterday. They'd come riding out of their distant nomadic past to found the greatest city in the world; and they were properly grateful to the bloodstock for making it possible. They even had some legend, I believe, about a mythical Great Horse of Asia, which would return to save them in time of peril. But apart from that, they had nothing that you or I would recognize as a god, within the meaning of the act.

So, when the TARDIS came groaning out of nowhere, of the three of us it was Hector who was the most put out; quite literally, in fact.

As he fell to his knees, dumbfounded by this immediate, unforseen acceptance of his challenge to Zeus, Achilles rallied sufficiently to run him through with a lance, or whatever. Very nasty, it was!

The thing pierced Hector's body in the region of the clavicle, I would imagine, and emerged, festooned with his internal arrangements, somewhere in the lumbar district. Blood and stuff everywhere, you know! I don't like to think of it.

Well, there's not a lot you can do about a wound like that – and Hector didn't. With a look of pained astonishment at being knocked out in the preliminaries by a despised and out-classed adversary, he subsided reluct-antly into the dust, and packed it in for the duration.

A great pity; because, by all accounts, he was an uncommonly decent chap at heart – fond of his dogs and children, and all that sort of thing. But there it is – you can't go barn-storming around, looking for trouble, and not expect to find it occasionally, that's what I say! Always taken very good care to avoid it myself... or at least, I had up till then. But I mustn't anticipate.

So – there lay Hector, his golden blood lacing his silver skin (and that's a phrase someone will pick up one day, I'll wager; but it was nothing like the foul reality, of course) when suddenly the door of the TARDIS opened and a little old man stepped out into the afternoon, blinking in the sunshine. And now it was Achilles' turn to fall to his knees...

At this point I must digress for a moment to explain that I have met the Doctor on several occasions since, and find him a most impressive character. But he didn't look so then, my word! I believe he has grown a great deal younger since, but at the time he looked – I hope he'll forgive me if he ever hears about this – he looked, I say, like the harassed captain of a coaster who can't remember his port from his starboard. A sort of superannuated Flying Dutchman, in fact: and not far out, at that, when you think about it.

I gathered later, that for some time the TARDIS had been tumbling origin over terminus through eternity, ricochetting from one more or less disastrous planetary landfall to another; when all the poor old chap wanted to do was get back to earth and put his feet up for a bit!

Well, he'd found the Earth all right, but unfortunately, several thousand miles and as many years from where he really wanted to be: which was, I gather, some place called London in the nineteen-sixties – if that means anything to you? He'd promised to give his friends, Vicki and Steven, a lift there, you see; because they thought it was somewhere they might be happy and *belong* for once. All very well for him, because *he* didn't truly belong anywhere – or, rather, he belonged everywhere; being a Time Lord, he claimed, or some such nonsense!

But the trouble was, he couldn't navigate, bless him! Oh, brilliant as the devil in his time, no doubt – whenever that *was* – but just a shade past it, if you ask me!

He blamed the mechanism of course – claimed it was faulty; but then don't they always? We've all heard it before – 'Damned sprockets on the blink!' or something; when all the time, if they're honest, they've completely forgotten what a sprocket is!

At all events, he was apparently under the impression

that he'd landed in the Kalahari Desert, and he was having a bit of trouble with the crew in consequence. So you can imagine his confusion when, expecting to be able to ask his way to the nearest water-hole from a passing bushman, he found himself being worshipped by a classical Greek hero, with, moreover, a Trojan warrior bleeding to death at his feet.

Achilles didn't help matters much by immediately addressing him as 'Father!' Disconcerting, to say the least.

'Eh? What's that? I'm not your father, my boy! Certainly not!' objected the Doctor, lustily. After all, Vicki and Steven were probably listening . . . 'This won't do at all – get up at once!'

Achilles was glad about that, you could tell. Sand burning his cuirasses, no doubt.

'If Zeus bids me rise, then must I do so . . .' He lumbered to his feet, rubbing his knees.

'Zeus?' enquired the Doctor, surprised. (And I must say he didn't look a lot like him.) 'What's this? Who do you take me for?'

'The father of the gods, and ruler of the world!' announced Achilles, clearing the matter up rather neatly.

'Dear me! Do you really? And may I ask, who you are?'

'I am Achilles – mightiest of warriors!' Yes, he could say that *now*. 'Greatest in battle, humblest of your servants.'

'I must say, you don't *sound* particularly humble! Achilles, eh? Yes, I've heard of you . . .'

Achilles looked pleased. 'Has my fame then spread even to Olympus? Tell me, I pray, what you have heard of me . . . ?'

Not an easy question to answer truthfully, but the Doctor did his best. 'Why, that you are rather . . . well, sensitive, shall we say? Or, perhaps, yes, well, never mind . . .' He gave up and changed the subject. 'And this poor fellow must be . . . ?'

'Hector, prince of Troy – sent to Hades for blasphemy

against the gods of Greece!'

'Blasphemy? Oh, really, Achilles – I'm sure he meant no particular harm by it!'

'Did he not? He threatened to trim your beard should you descend to earth!' He'd done nothing of the sort of course. Unpardonable.

'Did he indeed? But, as you see, I have no beard,' said the Doctor, putting his finger on the flaw in the argument.

'Oh, if you had appeared in your true form, I would have been blinded by your radiance! It is well known that when you come amongst us you adopt many different shapes. To Europa, you appeared as a bull, to Leda, as a swan; to me, you come in the guise of an old beggar ... !'

'I beg your pardon. I do nothing of the sort ...'

'But still your glory shines through!'

'So I should hope indeed ...'

Yes, but obviously such conversations cannot continue indefinitely, and the Doctor was aware of it. He began to shuffle, with dawning social embarrassment.

'Well, my dear Achilles, it has been most interesting to meet you ... but now, if you will excuse me, I really must return to my – er – my temple here. The others will be wondering about me.'

'The others?'

'Er – yes – the other gods, you understand? I have to be there to keep an eye on things, so I really should be getting back' And he turned to go.

With one of those leaps which I always think can do ballet-dancers no good at all, Achilles barred his way. 'No,' he barked, drawing his sword. The Doctor quailed, and one couldn't blame him. Gods don't expect that kind of thing.

'Eh?' he enquired, 'do you realize who you are addressing? Kindly let me pass. Before I – er, strike you with a thunderbolt!'

Achilles quailed in his turn. He didn't fancy that.

'Forgive me – but I must brave even the wrath of Zeus, and implore you to remain.'

Well, 'implore' yes – but still difficult, of course.

'I really don't see why I should. I have many other commitments, as I am sure you will appreciate...'

'And one of them lies here – in the camp of Agamemnon, our general! Hear me out, I pray: for ten long years we have laid siege to Troy, and still they defy us.'

'Well, surely, Achilles, now that Hector is dead...'

'What of that? Oh, they will be jubilant enough for a while, my comrades. Menelaus will drink too much, and songs will be sung in my honour. But our ranks have been thinned by pestilence, and the Trojan archers. There they sit, secure behind their walls, whilst we rot in their summers and starve in their crack-bone winters.'

All good stuff you see?

'Many of the Greeks will count the death of Hector enough. Honour is satisfied, they will say, and sail for home!'

Ever the pacifist the Doctor interrupted; 'Well, would that be such a bad idea?'

He wished he hadn't. Always a splashy speaker, Achilles now grew as sibilant as a snake...

'Lord Zeus, we fight in your name! Would you have the Trojan minstrels sing of how we fled before their pagan gods?'

The Doctor smiled patiently, wiping his face. 'Oh – I think you'll find Olympus can look after itself for a good many years yet...'

'Then come with me in triumph to the camp, and give my friends that message.'

Well, reasonable enough, you know, under the circumstances. And how the Doctor would have talked himself out of that one, we shall never know. Because just then the bushes behind them parted in a brisk manner, and out stepped a barrel-chested, piratical character, whose twinkling eyes and their sardonic accessories belied a

23

battle-scarred and weather-beaten body – which advanced with what I believe is called a nautical roll. He was followed by a band of obvious cut-throats, whom any sensible time traveller would have done well to avoid.

I suppose, at that time Odysseus would have been about forty-five.

4

Enter Odysseus

He and Achilles were technically on the same side, of course, but you could tell that neither of them was too happy about it. Different types of chap altogether. Achilles groaned inwardly; rather like Job, on learning that Jehovah's had another idea.

'What's this, Achilles?' Odysseus enquired, offensively. 'So far from camp, and all unprotected from a prisoner?'

Achilles made shushing gestures. 'This isn't a prisoner, Odysseus,' he said in tones of awestruck reverence.

'Certainly not,' contributed the Doctor, hastily.

'Not yet a prisoner? Then you should have screamed for assistance, lad; we wouldn't want to lose you. Come, let us see you home... Night may fall, and find thee from thy tent!'

'I'd resent his attitude, if I were you,' said the Doctor.

Odysseus spared him a scornful, cursory glance. 'Ah, but then, old fellow, you were *not* the Lord Achilles. He is not one to tempt providence, are you, boy?'

'Have a care, pirate!' warned Achilles, 'Are there no Trojan throats to slit, that you dare to tempt my sword?'

Odysseus considered the question, and came up with an undebatable answer. 'Throats enough, I grant you. A half score Trojans will not whistle easily tonight. We found 'em laughing by the ramparts, now they smile with their bellies. And what of you?' He wiped the evidence from his cutlass. 'Been busy have you?'

Achilles played his ace. 'Nothing to speak of,' he said

modestly, 'I met Prince Hector. There he lies.'

Astonished for once in his life, Odysseus noted the bleeding remains – and you could tell he was impressed. 'Zeus,' he exclaimed.

'Zeus *was* instrumental,' acknowledged Achilles gracefully, with a bow to the Doctor. Perhaps not surprisingly, the significance of this escaped Odysseus.

'No doubt,' he said, 'no doubt he was. But what a year this is for plague! The strongest must fall... Prince Hector, eh? Well, that he should come to this! You stumbled on him here, you say, as he lay dying?'

'I met him here in single combat, Odysseus.'

'The deuce you did? And fled him round the walls, till down he fell exhausted? A famous victory!'

'I met him face to face, I say,' scowled Achilles, stamping. 'I battled with him for an hour or more, until my greater skill o'ercame him! Beaten to his knees, he cried for mercy. Whereat I was almost moved to spare him...'

'Oh, bravo,' rumbled his appreciative audience.

Well, I could have said what really happened, of course, but I didn't like to interrupt – Achilles was all too obviously getting intoxicated by his talent for embroidery...

'But, mark this, Odysseus; as I was about to sheathe my sword in pity, there was a flash of lightning – and Lord Zeus appeared, who urged me on to strike.'

'And so, of course, you struck – like lightning? Well, boy – there, as you say, Prince Hector lies, and there your lance remains in seeming proof of it! I must ask your pardon...'

'So I should think,' hissed Achilles through pursed lips.

'But tell me, Lightfoot, what of Zeus? He intervened, I think you said? And then?'

'Why there he stands – and listens to your mockery.'

'Yes indeed, I've been most interested,' said the Doctor, getting a word in edgewise.

I wouldn't have advised it myself. A cut-throat or two did look vaguely apprehensive, but their leader rocked with the sort of laughter you hear in Athenian taverns at closing time.

'What, that old man? That thread-bare grey pate? Now, come, Achilles.'

'Odysseus, your blasphemy and laughter at the gods is very well in Ithaca. Think, though, before you dare indulge it here! Forgive him, Father Zeus – he is but a rough and simple sailor, who joined our holy cause for booty.'

'Aye, very rough, but scarce as simple as you seem to think!' growled the gallant captain, snapping a spear between his nerveless fingers.

'Oh, but there's nothing at all to forgive,' the Doctor hastened to assure him, 'I've no doubt he means well.'

'Then will you not come with us?' begged Achilles. Abject now, he was.

'Well, no – I hardly think . . . thank you, all the same . . .' Useless. Odysseus stumped forward, and siezed him by the scruff.

'What's that. You *will* come with us, man – or god, as I should say! If you indeed be Zeus, we have much need of your assistance! Don't cower there, lads. Zeus is on our side – or so Agamemnon keeps insisting. And since he has been so condescending as to visit us, bear him up, and carry him in triumph to the camp!'

The Doctor struggled, of course; but it was plainly no use. A bunch of tattooed ruffians tossed him aloft like a teetotum in a tantrum, and set him on their sweating shoulders. To do him credit, Achilles at least *objected*. 'Odysseus, I claim the honour to escort him! Let him walk to the camp with me!'

But not a bit of good did it do. Odysseus glowered like the Rock of Gibralter on a dull day. 'You shall have honour enough, lad, before the night's out. And, who knows? maybe we shall have a little of the truth as well. Father Zeus, we crave the pleasure of your company at supper. And perhaps a tale or two of Aphrodite, eh?'

The Doctor spluttered with indignation: 'Nothing

would induce me to indulge in vulgar bawdy!'

'Well then,' said Odysseus, reasonably, 'you will explain why you are lurking near the Graecian lines – and how you practised on the slender wits of young Achilles. That should prove equally entertaining.'

Rather foolishly, in my opinion, Achilles drew his sword. 'You will pay for this, Odysseus!' he shouted. The latter was unimpressed.

'Will I, Achilles? Well, we shall see . . . But meanwhile, lads, do some of you take up that royal carrion yonder. At least so much must we do for Lord Achilles, lest none believe his story. Nay, put up your sword, boy! We comrades should not quarrel in the sight of Zeus.'

And they marched away over the sky-line, carrying with them the helpless Doctor, and the mortal remains of Hector, Prince of Troy; while the echoes of Odysseus's laughter reverberated round the distant ramparts.

Achilles, for his part, looked – and, no doubt, felt – extremely foolish. At length, when the war-party was out of earshot, he spat after them: 'You will not laugh so loud, I think, when Agamemnon hears of this!'

Well, you have to say *something* don't you? Then he sprang nimbly off towards the Graecian lines by an alternative route. And, always having a nose for a good story, I followed at a more leisurely pace.

5

Exit the Doctor

Meanwhile, as they say, back in the TARDIS, the Doctor's situation was giving rise – as again they say – to serious concern. For, as they told me later, Vicki and Steven, his two companions, had been watching the progress, or rather, the retreat of events on the scanner, and they were pardonably worried. After all, he had only stepped out for a moment to enquire the way; and now, here he suddenly wasn't! You can imagine the conversation...

'They didn't look like aboriginal bushmen, Steven,' mused Vicki. 'Do you think this *is* the Kalahari Desert – or has he got it wrong again?'

'Of course he has!' snapped the irritated ex-astronaut. Sometimes he found Vicki almost as tiresome as the Doctor. After all, he hadn't joined the Space-Research Project to play the giddy-goat with Time as well! And if he didn't get back to base soon, awkward questions were gong to be asked. I mean, compassionate leave is one thing, but this was becoming ridiculous.

'If only,' he said, 'the Doctor would stop trying to pretend he's in control of events we might get somewhere! Why isn't he honest enough to admit that he has no idea how this thing operates? Then perhaps we could work out the basic principles of it together – after all, I do have a degree in science! But no – he's always got to know best, hasn't he? *Now* look at him – trussed like a chicken and being taken to God knows where!'

'Well, if they are bushmen,' said Vicki, looking on the

bright side, 'perhaps they've taken him to see their cave drawings?'

Steven regarded her with the sort of explosive pity one does well to avoid. 'Oh, do use what little sense I've tried to teach you! Those men were Ancient Greeks – that's who they were. Don't you remember *anything* from school? Its my belief we've gatecrashed into the middle of the Trojan War – and, if so, Heaven help us! Ten years that little episode lasted as I recall!'

'Well, whoever they were, they seemed to treat him with great respect...'

'Don't be silly, Vicki, they were laughing at him!'

'Yes,' she admitted, 'perhaps he made a joke?'

'If so, let's hope it was a practical one for a change! They didn't look as if they'd appreciate subtle humour...'

'I don't know, Steven... I thought the Greeks were civilized?'

'Only the later ones. I imagine these sort of people were little better than barbarians!'

'But I've always been told they were heroes. Magnificent men who had marvellous adventures. You know, like Jason and the Argonauts.'

'I'm afraid you've been reading too much mythology, Vicki – real life was never like that. But I suppose, in a sense, these characters would have been the original myth makers...'

'What do you mean?'

'I mean the ruffians whose rather shady little exploits were magnified by later generations, until they came to *seem* like heroes. But they were certainly nothing of the sort – and that's why I'm worried about the Doctor.'

'All right then, Steven. Have it your way. So, what can we do?'

'I know what I'm going to *have* to do, darn it, if we're ever to get out of this; follow them, and see if I can't rescue him before he gets his brilliant head cut off! Not that it wouldn't serve him right.'

'Well, can't I come too? If this *is* the Trojan War, I'd hate to miss it, and I'd love to see the real Agamemnon...'

Steven sighed. 'Yes – and no doubt he'd love to see you. You still don't understand, do you? Vicki, these people weren't gentlemen – and they certainy didn't treat women – even young girls – like ladies! No, you must stay here till I get back!'

'And what if you don't get back?'

'Thank you, Vicki – nice of you to think of that. Well, in that case, whatever you do, don't let yourself get taken prisoner. Just stay inside the TARDIS – and no one can get at you. You should be quite safe!'

'Yes, but supposing...'

'Look here, I haven't time to argue – just do as you're told for once!'

She watched him rebelliously, as he opened the double doors, her brain seething with mental reservations. But she said no more.

And Steven stepped out on to the plain of Scamander, took his bearings, and loped off after the rest of us.

6

A Rather High Tea

For some reason – not intentional, I assure you, – I
contrived to arrive at the Greek camp before the others.
Possibly Odysseus and his men had got themselves
involved in some more mayhem and casual butchery on
the way home – it would have been like them. And as for
Achilles, it may have been time for his evening press-ups
or something – but I really don't know. And it really
doesn't matter. At all events, I found it easy enough to
avoid the sentries, who didn't seem to be a very smart body
of men – playing skittles, most of them, with old thigh
bones and a skull which had seen better days; and pretty
soon I found myself outside the Commander's quarters –
the war-tent of Agamemnon.

And a fairly squalid sort of affair that was! Made, as far
as I could tell, of goat-skin – and badly cured goat-skin at
that – it flapped and sagged in the humid air, each
movement of the putrid pelts releasing an unmentionable
stench, which. one hoped, had nothing to do with the
evening meal! Because, as I could see through the open
tent-flap, Agamemnon himself and a dinner guest were
busily attacking the light refreshment with all the
disgusting gusto of a dormitory feast in a reform school.

And how did I know it was Agamemnon, you may ask?
It was impossible to mistake him – one has seen portraits,
of course, and heard the unsavoury stories: a great coarse
bully of a man, who looked as though he deserved every bit
of what was coming to him when he got home. Couldn't

happen to a nicer fellow! The Furies must have been off their heads, hounding his family the way they did. A justifiable homicide, if ever there was one, I'd say! But that, of course, is another story; and far off in the future, at that time.

No, it was Agamemnon all right: those rather vicious good looks and the body of an athlete run to seed look fine on the Mycenaean coins, but not in the flesh. And there was plenty of that in evidence; relaxed and unlaced as he was, after a hard day beating the living daylights out of the domestic help, I suppose, and generally carrying on. A sprinkling of the latter cowered cravenly in the offing, playing 'catch the ham-bone' amid a shower of detritus which the master tossed tidily over his shoulder, while otherwise engaged in putting the fear of god into Menelaus.

For that's who his companion was, without a doubt; apart from an unfortunate family resemblance, there was a wealth of sibling feeling concealed in their gruff remarks.

'You drink too much,' belched Agamemnon, with his mouth full – or at least, it had been full before he spoke. Now ... well, never mind. 'Why can't you learn to behave more like a king, instead of a dropsical old camp follower? Try to remember you're my brother, and learn a little dignity.'

Blearily, Menelaus uncorked himself from a bottle of the full-bodied Samoan. 'One of the reasons I drink, Agamemnon, is to forget that I'm your brother! Ever since we were boys, you've dragged me backwards to fiasco – and this disastrous Trojan escapade takes the Bacchantes' bath-salts for incompetence! If not the Gorgon's hair-net,' he added, anxious to clinch the matter with a telling phrase. 'Ten foul years we've been here, and ... well, I'm not getting any younger. I want to go home!'

'You won't get a lot older if you take that tone with me – brother or no brother! What's the matter with you, man? Don't you want to see Helen again? Don't you want to get your wife back?'

'Now I'm glad you asked me that – because, quite frankly, no, I don't. And if you'd raised the point before, you'd have saved us a great deal of trouble. If you want to know, I was heartily glad to see the back of her.'

Agamemnon looked shocked. 'You shouldn't talk like that in front of the servants,' he said, lowering his voice to a bellow.

'Well, it wasn't the first time she'd let herself be – shall we say – abducted?' said Menelaus, raising his to a whisper. 'There was that awful business with Hercules, remember? And if we ever do get her back, I'll wager it won't be the last time either. I can't keep on rushing off to the ends of the Earth after her. Makes me a laughing stock...' He recorked himself, moodily.

'Now, you knew perfectly well what she was like before you married her. I warned you at the time, no good would come of it. But since you were so besotted as not to listen, it became a question of honour to get her back. Of *family* honour, you understand?'

'Not to mention King Priam's trading concessions, of course! You're just making my marriage problems serve your political ambitions. Think I don't know?'

Agamemnon sighed deeply. The effect was unpleasant, even at a range of several yards. Candle flames trembled, and sank back into their sockets: as did his brother's blood-shot eyes. 'There may be some truth in that,' he admitted, 'I don't say there is, but there may be. However, I must remind you that these ambitions would have been served just as well if you had killed Paris in single combat, as was expected of you. That's what betrayed husbands do, damn it! They kill their wife's lovers. Everybody knows that. And Paris was quite prepared to let the whole issue be decided by such a contest – he told me so. So don't blame me because you've dragged us into a full scale war – because I won't have it.'

Menelaus looked aggrieved. 'But I *did* challenge him, if you remember? First thing I did when I noticed she'd gone! Ten rotten years ago! And the fellow wouldn't accept.'

'True,' said Agamemnon, giving a grudging nod with a chin or two. 'So you did, and so he wouldn't. He's as cowardly as you are!'

'Once and for all, I am not a coward! I wish you wouldn't keep on.'

'Well, if you're such a fire-eater, why don't you challenge someone else, then – if only for the look of the thing? Why not challenge Hector, for instance?'

In a vain attempt to increase his stature, Menelaus staggered to his feet, 'Are you demented? Not even Ajax would go against Hector, it would be suicide!'

'Now you don't know till you've tried, do you?' asked his brother, reasonably. 'I think this is a very good idea of yours. Tell you what, I shall issue the challenge first thing in the morning on your behalf. That will lend credibility, won't it?'

And no doubt he would have done, too. Menelaus obviously thought so, and blanched beneath his pallor to prove it.

But at this moment Achilles made the entrance for which he'd been rehearsing. He had wisely discarded any elaborate form of words in favour of the simple, dramatic announcement: 'Hector is dead!' – and he waited stauesquely for his well-earned applause.

To his surprise, he didn't get it. Mind you, Menelaus did mop his brow and sink back on his quivering buttocks: but Agamemnon's reaction was perhaps not all that could have been desired by a popular hero of the hour. Generals are not used to having their master-plans so abruptly rebuffed . . . He tapped the table with a fist like diseased pork.

'When?' he inquired irritably. 'How in Hades did that happen?'

'This afternoon,' explained Achilles, rather lamely – his whole effect spoiled. 'I slew him myself, after an hour or so of single combat,' he added hopefully, trying to recapture the original impetus.

'Oh, you did, did you? Well, congratulations, of course. Still – there's another good idea wasted!'

'What do you mean "wasted"?' pouted the understandably crestfallen combatant; 'Here, have I been wearing my sandals to shreds . . .'

'Yes, yes, yes – of course you have,' agreed Agamemnon, too late for comfort, 'it's just that Menelaus here was about to challenge him, weren't you? Well, now we'll just have to think of something else for him to do, damn it! Still, you mustn't think I'm not pleased with you, because I am. You've done very well – better than anybody could have expected. So, why don't you sit down and tell us about it?'

'If you don't mind,' said Achilles, rather stiffly, 'I think I'd prefer to make my report officially, tomorrow morning – before our assembled forces, if that could be managed.'

'I suppose something might be organized on those lines . . .'

'But for the moment, I have other more important news!'

'More important than the death of Hector? What a busy day you've been having, to be sure. Go on, then.'

Achilles took a deep breath. This, you could tell he felt, was the high spot. 'At the height of my battle with Hector, there came a sudden lightning flash, and Father Zeus appeared before me!'

There was a silence, during which Menelaus spilled his wine. 'Eh?' he enquired nervously.

'It's all right, Menelaus,' comforted his brother, 'he's been listening to too much propaganda, haven't you Achilles? Mind you, I don't say we couldn't use a story like that – it's quite a good notion in fact. But you mustn't go taking that sort of thing seriously – or you'll lose the men's respect.'

'But it's true, I tell you!' said Achilles, stamping petulantly, 'He appeared from nowhere, in the shape of a little old man . . .'

Agamemnon considered. One had *heard* of these cases, of course. 'Hmm . . . did he, indeed? And where is he now, this little old man of yours?'

'I'm afraid I have to report that Odysseus and his men took him prisoner!'

Now it was Agememnon's turn to attempt the leaping to the feet routine. He succeeded only partially – then thought better of it, and did the table-thumping trick again instead. 'They did *what*?'

'Odysseus mocked him. Then they seized him – and they're dragging him back here now. I ran ahead to warn you . . .'

'You did well.' Recognition at last! 'Perdition take Odysseus! After all, you can't be too careful these days. It *may*, in fact, *be* Zeus – and then where would we all be?'

'Precisely,' agreed Menelaus, taking another large gulp of his medicine.

'*May* be Zeus?' trumpeted Achilles, indignantly, 'I tell you, he appeared out of thin air, complete with his temple.'

'Oh, he would do – that's what he does!' moaned Menelaus. 'Heaven help us!'

'Be quiet, Menelaus!' said Agamemnon. 'Guard, go seek the Lord Odysseus and command his presence here.'

But it wasn't a good day for Agamemnon; for the second time in as many minutes, his initiative was frustrated by events. Even as the guard struggled to attention, preparatory to completing his esteemed order, Odysseus himself barrelled through the tent-flap.

'Command?' he questioned, bubbling with menace, 'who dares command Odysseus?' And he flung the good Doctor into the centre of the appreciative audience before him.

7

Agamemnon Arbitrates

It was not, perhaps, the dignified entrance the Doctor
would have chosen, left to himself; but with his usual
resilience, he determined to make the best of a bad job.
Rather neatly he did it too, in my opinion.

'Exactly!' he said, before Agamemnon could attempt to
stand on ceremony, 'That is what I should like to know!
Who *is* in command round here?'

Absolutely the right tone, under the circumstances –
because so unexpected, you see? And you could tell
Agamemnon was somewhat disconcerted by it.

'I ... er ... that is to say, I have that honour,' he replied
defensively.

'Ah, just so. Then you, I take it, are Agamemnon?'

'Well, most people, you know, call me *Lord* Agamemnon – but let that pass for the moment.'

'I would prefer to – at least until we see whether you are
worthy of the title.'

'Most people find it advisable to take that for granted.'

'Dear me, do they now? Then perhaps you will explain
why this mountebank, Odysseus, presumes to be a law
unto himself – insults your guests, and even dares to laugh
at Zeus?'

'Careful, dotard!' rumbled Odysseus. 'It seems,' he said
to the company at large, 'that times upon Olympus are not
what they were, and gods must go a-begging.'

The remark had a mixed reception: Menelaus, for
instance, got under the table, while Achilles looked angry

and Agamemnon thoughtful.

'Odysseus will be reprimanded,' he conceded. 'If, that is, you are who you say you are.'

'Should that make any difference? Whether I be god or man, I come to you in peace.'

'Quite so. But if I may inquire, with all respect, which are you?' Not wishing to commit himself at this point, the Doctor passed the buck.

'Didn't Achilles tell you?'

'Achilles is a good lad, but impressionable. Whereas Odysseus, with all his faults, is a man of the world, and perceptive with it – and he seems to disagree. Now, you see my quandary? I suppose I can hardly ask for your credentials, can I?'

'I would not advise it,' said the Doctor, hastily, 'I suggest, however that you treat with me honour – as befits a stranger.'

Achilles was feeling a bit left out of things, and tried to grab some of the action. 'Of course he's right – of course we must – and it's what I've been *trying* to do. Fools, don't you see, he's Zeus and he's come to help us?'

A good try – but he still hadn't won the meeting over, not by a long sight. The Doctor knew it, and made what he took to be a shrewd point.

'Look here, suppose for a moment that I *were* an enemy, then what could one man do, alone, against the glory that is Greece, eh?'

'A neat phrase,' admitted Agamemnon.

'And a good point,' added his brother, confirming the Doctor's opinion and emerging cautiously from hiding.

'Which only you would be fool enough to take,' snarled Odysseus, out of patience. 'The man is a spy! Deal with him – and be brief, or I shall undertake it for you!'

Achilles bounded forward, in that impetuous way of his. 'After I am dead, Odysseus, and only then!'

Odysseus could make a concession, if he had to. 'If you insist,' he smiled, 'I shall be happy to oblige you, giant killer.'

But Agamemnon lurched mountainously between them. 'Silence, both of you! This needs further thought, not sword-play.'

'Then since my thoughts seem to be of such little account,' said Odysseus, 'allow me to withdraw. I for one, want no dealings with the gods – I need a breath of pagan air!'

And he stormed out into the night, to the relief of the rest of those present. Only Achilles seemed inclined to pursue the matter, and knelt at the Doctor's feet, almost cringing with unsought servility.

'Father Zeus, I ask your pardon, the man is a boor. If you command me I will let the pagan air he values into his blasphemous guts.'

'Oh, do get up, my dear fellow, there's a good chap,' said the Doctor embarassed. 'No, Achilles – whether he knows it or not, Odysseus is one of my most able servants. He is the man who will shortly bring about Troy's downfall.' (He must have read my book, you see? Which, of course, I hadn't written at the time.) 'So it would be stupid to kill him now, wouldn't it? When you are almost within sight of victory?'

This, of course, went down very well, as he must have known it would. Agamemnon beamed incredulously. 'What – do you prophesy as much?'

'I can almost guarantee it,' said the Doctor recklessly.

'Almost?'

'Well, may I ask, first of all, what my position here is to be? Am I to be treated as a god or as a spy? I may say that I shall not remain unbiased by your decision. Not that you *can* kill me, of course,' he added cunningly, 'but it you were foolish enough to attempt it, it could easily cost you the war.'

Agamemnon pondered the logic of this. 'Yes, I quite see. But on the other hand, if we *don't* kill you, and then you prove to be a spy after all, the same thing might happen, so you must appreciate my dilemma. What do you think Menelaus?'

'I don't know,' quavered the abject latter. 'I wish I did, but I don't. Either prospect terrifies me. Can't we arrive at a compromise?'

'Kill him just a little, you mean? Typically spineless advice, if I may say so! But for once, I'm afraid you're probably right!' He turned to the interested Doctor. 'Yes, having looked at the thing from all angles, I propose to place you under arrest.'

'Arrest? How dare you? You'll be sorry, I promise you that!'

'Yes, I suppose I may be – but we must risk it. And it will be a very reverent arrest, of course. In fact, if you prefer, I could describe it as a probationary period of cautious worship. So you mustn't be offended. After all, most gods are, to some extent, the prisoners of their congregations. And meanwhile we shall hope to enjoy the benefits of your experience and advice, whilst you are enjoying our hospitality. How about that?'

The Doctor made the best of it, as usual. He could hardly do otherwise. 'Very well, that sounds most acceptable,' he said, 'even attractive. Thank you.'

'Excellent! Then do sit down and have a ham-bone.'

And there for the moment the matter rested. Or rather, seemed to.

8

An Execution is Arranged

Because, of course, Odysseus had only *seemed* to storm off into the middle distance. For he was never a man to let his judgement be clouded by controversy, however boisterous, and he had been much struck by the Doctor's claiming to be a man alone – and therefore harmless.

He didn't believe for a moment that the Doctor *was* harmless, and therefore assumed logically that he was probably *not* alone, either. And he felt he should have thought of that before – and went scouring the night for the support forces.

It was this sort of reasoning which made him the most dangerous of all the Greek captains; this, and an arrogant independence of spirit which made it difficult at times to diagnose his motives, or to forecast which way he would jump in a crisis.

Well, on this occasion it was Steven he jumped on. Personally, I was well concealed in a clump of cactus I wasn't too fond of; but Steven had elected to climb into a small tree, where he looked ridiculously conspicuous against the rising moon, rather like a 'possum back on the old plantation. And the hound-dog had him in no time at all.

Oh, a well set-up fellow Steven may have been, who'd done his share of amateur athletics during training, but he was patently no match for Odysseus who was like nothing you'd meet in the second eleven on a Saturday knock-about. So he was hauled from his perch in very short order

42

and with scant ceremony.

'So, what have we here?' said the hero, grinning like a hound-dog that had thought as much. 'Another god, perhaps?'

You couldn't blame Steven for not rising to the occasion as he might have done had the circumstances been different – and if he'd known what Odysseus was talking about.

'I am a traveller,' he announced, lamely. 'I had lost my way, and I saw the light.'

Very likely, I must say. He didn't look as if he'd seen the light. Odysseus snorted, to indicate his opinion of this closely reasoned alibi.

'Come,' he said, having concluded the snort, 'at least you are the god Apollo to walk invisible past sentries?'

Steven attempted injured innocence. 'What sentries?' he inquired, 'I saw no sentries.'

'Did you not? Well, maybe they are sleeping – and with a knife between their ribs, I'll wager! Shall we go seek them together? Or would that be a foolish waste of time? Well, the light attracted you, you say? Then little moth, go singe your wings.'

Of course, no twelve stone man likes to be called 'little moth' – but there's not much he can do about it, if he's hurtling through a tent-flap, like an arrow from a bow. So he let the remark pass for the moment, and presently found himself in the centre of a circle of surprised but interested faces – one of whom, he was glad to notice, was the Doctor. Nevertheless – difficult, the whole thing.

'And who is it this time?' asked Agamemnon, reasonably enough. His tea was being constantly interrupted by one air-borne, hand-hurled stranger after another.

Odysseus positively purred with complacent triumph. 'My prisoner, the god Apollo,' he announced, smiling. So might Pythagoras have murmured QED, on finding he could balance an equation with the best of them. 'Achilles, will you not worship him? Fall to your knees? He is, of course, another Trojan spy – but of such undoubted divinity that he must be spared.' He was enjoying his little moment. Steven did his best to spoil it for him.

'I'm not a Trojan,' he asserted firmly, 'I did tell you I'm a traveller – well, a sort of traveller – and I lost my way.'

Well, it did get a laugh, but not the sort he wanted, by any means. Sarcastic, it was. They looked as if they'd heard that one before. In danger, he realised, of losing his audience, he appealed to the Doctor. 'Look here, you seem to have made friends quickly enough. Fxplain who I am, can't you?'

'Ah,' chirruped Odysseus, 'so you *do* know each other then? In that case no further explanation is necessary. You must certainly be from Olympus and the gods are always welcome. I ask your pardon. Drop in any time.'

'Well,' enquired Agamemnon of the Doctor, packing a wealth of menace into the syllable, 'have you nothing to say?'

Surprisingly, especially to Steven, the Doctor looked puzzled.

'I have never seen this man before in my life!' he lied stoutly, with a dismissive wave of his ham-bone, 'He is, of course, merely trying to trick you.'

Steven, for his part, looked as if he'd aways expected his ears sometimes to deceive him – and now his friends were adopting the same policy.

'How can you sit there,' he stammered, 'and deny –' Words failed him, and just as well too, because Agamemnon had heard quite enough of them to be going on with . . .

'Silence,' he barked, clarifying this position. 'Take him away, Odysseus. Why must I be troubled with every petty, pestilential prisoner? First cut out his tongue for insolence, then make an end!'

But Odysseus was after bigger game. 'Softly now. Suppose we are mistaken, and the man *is* just an innocent traveller, as he told us? I could never sleep easily again, were I to kill him while any doubt remained. Remorse would gnaw at my vitals – and I wouldn't want that. All-seeing Zeus – this man who presumptiously claimed your friendship... is he a spy or not?'

The Doctor looked bored with the whole subject. 'I neither know nor care. I must say, it looks very much as if he is.'

'And shall he be put to death?'

'I would strongly advise it,' recommended the Doctor, blandly, 'it would be very much safer, on the whole. Can't be too careful, can you?'

An air of business having been concluded pervaded the meeting. Open season on spies having been declared, Achilles and Odysseus, unanimous for once, drew their swords and advanced on the wretched Steven.

At which point, the Doctor rose imperiously. 'Stop,' he commanded not a moment too soon, 'Have you lost your senses the pair of you?' The two heroes paused in mid-execution.

'Ah, now we have it,' grinned Odysseus, 'On second thoughts, Zeus decides we should release him to return to Troy!'

'Do not mock me, Lord Odysseus! What, would you stain the tent of Agamemnon with a Trojan's blood?'

Personally, I didn't think one stain more or less would be noticed, but rhetoric must be served, I suppose, and the Doctor warmed to his theme accordingly. 'I claim this quavering traitor as a sacrifice to Olympus! Bring him therefore to my temple in the plain at sunrise tomorrow, and then I will show you a miracle!'

Here he contrived a covert wink at Steven, who seemed to think it was about time for something of the sort.

'A miracle, eh?' mused Odysseus. 'Well, that, of course, would be most satisfactory.' Even Menelaus perked up, and looked quite excited at the prospect.

'Conclusive proof, I would say,' he judged; and then spoilt it all by adding, 'of something or other.'

But Agamemnon wanted tomorrow's programme itemised. 'And exactly what sort of miracle do you intend to show us?' he enquired.

The Doctor improvized... 'Why – I shall – er – I shall strike him with a thunderbolt from Heaven! That'll teach him!'

'Oh, very spectacular!' approved Odysseus. 'Well, we shall see. Our weather is so unpredictable. And tomorrow, if there is no thunder on the plain, I have a sword will serve for two, as well as one.'

As if to confirm his doubts, the next day dawned to a heavy drizzle. But you can't beat a good public execution for box-office; and in spite of the rain, quite a crowd of those concerned assembled to enjoy the spectacle.

The two principals, Steven and the Doctor, were there, of course. And both Agamemnon and Odysseus were in close support, together with a motley assemblage of the brutal and licentious, come to see the fun.

But Achilles wasn't there – he was sulking in his tent again, having had his triumph postponed in favour of the major attraction.

And Menelaus wasn't – he had a hangover.

And one other essential item was missing: not a temple of Zeus was to be seen anywhere!

Overnight the TARDIS had vanished.

9

Temple Fugit

At first, the Doctor and Steven took the panic-stricken
assumption that Vicki had somehow dematerialized the
TARDIS, by sitting down on the control panel, or
something; but, in fact, she had done nothing of the sort –
and just as well for everybody.

No, at that very moment, the poor child was being
shaken about like a ticket in a tombola, as Prince Paris and
a patrol of Trojans trundled the time-machine into Troy,
as spoils of war!

Somehow they had contrived to get the thing up onto
rollers, and were bumping it along in a way that boded no
good to its already erratic mechanism – or to Vicki's either,
come to that.

But, of course, we weren't to know that at the time, and
the Doctor looked as foolish as a conjuror, who, about to
produce the promised rabbit, discovers he's left it in his
other hat!

'It should be somewhere here,' he temporized. 'Or
perhaps further to the left... it's extremely hard to say.
These sand-hills are so much alike...'

'Or, perhaps, Father Zeus, the weight of centuries has
made you absent-minded?' suggested Odysseus, nastily.
'You're quite sure, now, that you ever had a temple?'

'Of course I had, you must have seen it yourself! Every
god has a temple, has to have, or people stop believing in
you in no time...'

'Precisely my point. And what I saw yesterday didn't

47

strike me as being particularly ecclesiastical. More like a sort of rabbit-hutch,' he explained to the others.

'Nothing of the sort! Ask Achilles, if you don't believe me; he saw it materialize.'

'So he said. But then, Achilles will say anything to be the centre of attention. In any case, unfortunately for you, he's not here. No doubt he felt he'd championed a losing cause and held it tactful to be absent.'

The skies had blown clear by now, but not before the rains had softened the ground, and Agamemnon was casting about for tracks, like an over-weight boar-hound. '*Something* has been here,' he admitted, indicating the furrows in the mud, left by the TARDIS, 'Look ...'

'Aye, and someone, too,' agreed Odysseus, 'some several tracks which lead across to Troy! Enough of this foolishness! Your friends in the city have doubtless thought your ruse successful, and reclaimed their own.'

'They've captured it, you mean,' contradicted the Doctor, 'you must help me to get it back – and at once.'

'And walk into a trap, of course? Yes, you'd like that I'm sure. Admit your fault. Lord Agamemnon, these men are *both* spies.'

'So it would begin to seem,' said the general, reluctantly. 'Very well, bring forward the prisoner. Now, Father Zeus, – you have but one chance left to prove yourself. Kill this Trojan, as you promised.'

Odysseus tapped a sandal impatiently. 'Yes, fling a thunderbolt – or do something to rise to the occasion.'

The Doctor was beginning to run out of steam. 'But I tell you, the sacrifice can only be performed *within* the temple. Didn't I mention that?'

'Yes, yes, yes ... which temple is now in Troy, and therefore will we give you leave to go there? Just so. Well, I, for one, have heard enough. Perhaps Lord Agamemnon here will still believe ... until he reads your war memoirs.'

The game was obviously up, and the Doctor knew it. He looked at the vicious circle of angry, disbelieving faces and he smiled sadly. 'Yes, quite so. There is no need to labour the point. I am not Zeus, of course, and this man *is* my friend. But I ask you to believe that neither of us is a Trojan.'

Brave of him, I thought, but his honesty proved useless.

'I care not who you are,' roared Agamemnon. 'Seize him! It is enough that you have trifled with my credulity, and made me look a fool, in front of my captains.'

'Oh, don't say that,' soothed Odysseus, pouring oil on troubled flames. 'Rest assured we shall never hold it against you. A song or two, perhaps, about the fire, telling how Agamemnon dined with Zeus, and begged a Trojan prisoner for advice. But nothing detrimental!'

Agamemnon controlled himself with the difficulty he always experienced. 'Well – very well, Odysseus, enjoy your little joke. I shall not forget your part in this – you brought them both to camp, remember! Now, finish the business, and be brief. And do not bring their bodies back. Let them rot here, disembowelled and unburied, as a gift to the blow-flies and a warning to their fellows...'

'Aye, in a very little while, O great commander. But first, Lord of men, since we have two Trojans all alive, may I not question them? Just a formality, of course, unimportant trifles, like their army's present strength and future plans.'

'As you wish. Drag what information you can from them, and as painfully as possible. Then report to me – and don't delay. The sun is up; patrols are out, and, much as I might welcome it myself, we can't afford to lose you – at the moment!'

'You are very kind,' smiled Odysseus, with a mocking bow; and Agamemnon splashed angrily off through the mud, at the head of his sniggering soldiers.

Odysseus watched them go. Then, turning to his two terrified prisoners, he drew his great bronze sword, and wiped it thoughtfully on his sleeve.

They watched the manoeuvre with fascinated horror. He plucked a hair from his beard, and tested it appraisingly on the blade's edge. It fell in two, without a detectable struggle. They closed their eyes and waited for the end.

'It's all right,' said Odysseus, 'I was only going to lean on it.' He did so, folding his tattooed arms on the ornate hilt.

They opened their eyes, wondering if perhaps there was a future to face after all. 'And now then, mannikins, first of all, tell me who you *really* are!'

I told you he was different from all the other Greeks, didn't I? You never knew *where* you were with Odysseus.

10

The Doctor Draws a Graph

'But I thought you'd already made up your mind who we are,' said Steven, after a surprised pause. 'Trojan spies, I think you said?'

Odysseus laughed, in that sabre-toothed, ceramic-shattering way of his. 'Aye – and so at first I thought. And so, later, I was content to have that fool, Agamemnon, believe.'

'Well, I'm glad you've revised your opinion,' said the Doctor. 'So who do you think we are now?'

'I do not know. Your costume is not Trojan, and your posturing as Zeus was so absurd, I do not think Trojan wit could sink so low.'

'I did not posture. How dare you! I merely met Achilles, and...'

'He thrust the role upon you? This I can believe. That muscle-bound body-building Narcissus fears his shadow in the sunshine, will not so much as comb his hair until he reads the new day's auguries. He is so god-fearing that he sees them everywhere – and trembles at 'em all. But I am not Achilles... No, and you are not a Trojan. So, I ask again, who are you?'

'I think we'd better tell him, Doctor,' said Steven.

'A doctor now? Hippocrates are you? Have a care...'

'Nothing of the sort – I am a doctor of science not medicine.'

'A doctor of what?' enquired Odysseus, puzzled.

'Oh, dear me, this is obviously going to take some time. I

51

mean, if I have to keep defining my terms.'

'Define what you like – but remember the terms are mine not yours! And I shall be patient. Only this time, if you value your lives, do not lie to me.'

So the Doctor began to explain about the TARDIS. A difficult task, obviously, because how do you describe a time-machine to a man who has never even heard of Euclid, never mind Einstein? Of course, up till then, I'd never heard of them myself, but I must say I found the whole concept fascinating. Odysseus however seemed to be labouring somewhere between incredulity and incomprehension, and only brightened up when they came to the stories about their previous adventures – which he naturally would, being something of an adventurer himself.

Nevertheless a longship isn't a TARDIS by any means, and personally I wouldn't have bet much on their chances of being believed, or of getting away with their skins in the sort of condition they would wish. I think the Doctor realized this, and eventually ground to a somewhat stammering standstill, leaving Steven to wind things up: '... and so really, we arrived in your time, Odysseus, quite by accident. Just another miscalculation of the Doctor, here.'

'I wouldn't call it a miscalculation, my boy! In fact, with all eternity to choose from, I think a margin of error of a century or so is quite understandable. No, I think I've done rather well to get us to Earth at all!'

'I'm glad you're so pleased with yourself! I suppose I should be grateful for being about to have my throat cut?'

Odysseus turned from a space-time graph which the Doctor had drawn in the sand, and erased it scornfully with his foot. 'Now, now, no one has mentioned cutting throats!'

'Of course they haven't,' said the Doctor, seizing on the vital point.

'No,' continued Odysseus, reassuringly, 'I had something rather more painful in mind – painful and lingering for the both of you.' He scowled. 'As it is, however, I haven't quite decided.'

If the Doctor had a fault, it was that he never knew when to leave well alone. Interested in everything, he was. 'Some form of ritual death, no doubt? That is quite customary, I believe, among primitive peoples. Fascinating.'

'Doctor, will you please be quiet? I'm afraid I don't share your admirable scientific detachment! Listen, Odysseus; my friend didn't mean to imply that you were primitive.'

The hero roused himself from his reverie. 'Didn't he? Oh, but I am – extremely primitive! I have none of the urban sophistication of my friend, Agamemnon. In fact, some people have gone so far as to call me an uncouth, barbarian pirate! They haven't lived long afterwards, mark you, but they've said it. And they were quite right. That, perhaps, is why I am tempted to believe you.'

'Well, I really don't see why you shouldn't,' said the Doctor, 'it's all quite true.'

'Possibly it is. I have travelled far in my life upon what you would probably call deplorable adventures. And they have brought me into contact with a great many deplorable persons who have told me various outrageous stories of myths and monsters. But not one of them has had the effrontery to strain my credulity as you have done. Therefore, I think your story is *probably* true – otherwise you could not have dared to tell it. And so, I propose to release you.'

'Well,' said Steven, relieved, 'I think that's very nice of you.'

'Oh, no, it isn't! You haven't heard what I have in mind for you yet. There are, you see, certain conditions.'

'Conditions, indeed!' said the Doctor, 'And what, pray are they?'

'Why, that you use this almost supernatural power of yours to devise a scheme for the capture of Troy!'

'But I'm afraid I can't do that! Oh, no – I make it a rule never to meddle in the affairs of others!'

'Then I would advise you to break it on this occasion.'

'So would I,' gulped Steven.

'Quite so. You see, I am getting more than a little tired of this interminable war. My wife, Penelope, will never believe that it has lasted *this* long. So already I had half decided to sail for home; but it does seem a pity to have wasted all this time, without so much as a priceless Trojan goblet to show for it. I promised the boys booty, and booty they shall have! So I am going to give you forty-eight hours to think of something really ingenious.'

'Two days?' calculated the Doctor, gulping in his turn. 'That isn't long...'

'It should be enough if you are as clever as you say you are.'

Ever the realist, Steven asked, 'What happens if we fail?'

'I shouldn't enquire if I were you. It would only upset you. Because if you fail, I shall have been foolish to have believed your story, and I would hate to be made to seem a fool. I should be very, very angry.'

As he said this, Odysseus sliced through their bonds with a backhand sweep of his cutlass, and then drove his two protesting prisoners back the way they had come.

It seemed pointless to follow them for the moment. I had learned quite enough astonishing new facts for one morning, and I wanted to digest the implications.

I mean, if time travel were really possible, why – what a collaborator the Doctor would make. Already half a dozen ideas for new books were clamouring for attention in my reeling mind – science fiction, I thought I might call them; at least, until a better notion occurred.

Besides, I thought it was time for *somebody* to see what might be happening *inside* the city of Troy for a change. How would they cope with a time-machine, I wondered.

So, I went to find out.

11

Paris Draws the Line

It wasn't as difficult to get into Troy as you might suppose, considering all the heavy weather the Greeks were making of it. However to be fair, I have to admit that an army is one thing and an inconspicuous, casually dressed poet, quite another.

At all events, I arrived outside the main gates – very impressive they were, I must say – solid bronze by the look of them, with brass ornamentations, just as Prince Paris and his men were man-handling the TARDIS through there.

Considering all the stertorous breathing, groaning and so forth that was going on, I calculated that they might be glad of some assistance, however modest; so I rolled up my sleeves and lent a shoulder. No one so much as raised an eyebrow; in fact, I was cheerfully accepted as a colleague by one and all. And in no time, there we were in the main square, the gates were barred and bolted behind us, and a crowd of miscellaneous spectators were giving us a bit of a cheer. Nothing to it.

Except that – my word! – the thing was as heavy as lead, and *that* removed any doubts I might have had about the Doctor's story. Quite obviously, there was far more of it inside, then met the eye from outside – if you follow me? So we were all extremely glad to set it down.

Prince Paris was pleased with himself no end – you could tell that! He strutted about the little building like a peacock in full courtship display. Well, he could afford to;

he hadn't been doing a lot of work, and wasn't as fagged out as the rest of us.

But an interesting looking man, all the same. By no means a bully-boy, like his deceased elder brother, and with what I believe is called a sensitive face. Intelligent, anyway – and I wondered if half the stories one heard about him were true.

He didn't look like a debauchee – far from it. No, more like an unwilling conscript, prepared to make the best of things for the sake of family tradition, and all that. The sort of man you wouldn't at all have minded having a drink with – except that it would have been a reasonable bet that he'd have left his money in his other uniform.

Anyway, it was obvious at the moment, that he thought he'd pulled off rather a coup. 'Halt!' he commanded, shortly after we'd just done so. 'Cast off the ropes, there!' Yes, we'd done that as well. So he thought for a moment, and added, 'Sound the trumpets!'

Well, that was new, at any rate, and after a short pause, while the surprised warriors fumbled about for the instruments, knocked the moths, fluff et cetera out of them, the most God-awful noise broke out. A fanfare of sorts, I took it to be, and possibly just the thing to stiffen the sinews – if you hadn't been up all night, downwind of Agamemnon's tent, as I had.

As it was, I couldn't take it at that hour in the morning, and I scurried away to suitable cover. Nobody had thanked me for my help, but you don't really expect that these days. And as I cowered behind a giant pilaster with flowered finials, or whatever it was – a great stone column anyway, outside what I took to be the palace, another light sleeper emerged.

'What is it now?' King Priam asked irritably. 'By the Great Horse of Asia is none of us to rest? Who's there?'

You could sense at once that he was a Trojan of the old school, accustomed to getting his own way, or knowing the reason why. In his mid-sixties, I should think, but well-preserved and still formidable.

Paris pranced proudly forwards, like a war-horse saying 'ha-ha!' to the trumpets: 'It's Paris, father, returned from patrol.'

'Well, why can't you do it *quietly*? What news, boy? Have you avenged your brother, Hector, yet? Have you killed Achilles?'

'Ah,' said Paris, 'I sought Achilles, father, even to the Graecian lines. I flung my challenge at him, but he skulked within his tent and feared to face me.'

A likely story, I must say, and not at all good enough, as it proved.

'Well, you go back and wait until he gets his courage up! Upon my soul, what sort of brother are you? And, furthermore, what sort of son?' He noticed the TARDIS for the first time. 'What's that you've got there?'

'A prize, father, captured from the Greeks.'

'Captured, you say? I should think they were glad to see the back of it. What is it?'

Paris had been rather afraid of that. He wasn't sure – and you couldn't blame him. But he did his best. 'It's a sort of shrine, it seems . . .'

'And what, may I ask, do you propose to do with this seeming shrine?'

Paris tilted his helmet over one eye, and scratched his head. 'You don't like it where it is?'

'I do not. Right in everybody's way! How are the chariots meant to get around it?'

'Ah, I hadn't thought of that.'

'Think about it now.'

'Right ho! Then how about if we put it in the temple?'

Not a bad solution, I'd have thought, but at this moment there was an interruption to the steady flow of reasoned argument.

'You are *not* putting that thing in my temple,' snarled a shrill voice from the opposite side of the square, and there was Paris's sister, Cassandra, standing on the steps of the temple in question.

A bad woman to cross, Cassandra; put me in mind of her

57

brother Hector in drag, if you can imagine such a thing. Paris quailed before her.

'Ah, there you are,' he said. 'Well, the point is, old thing, Father and I were rather hoping, we could, perhaps...'

'Nothing of the kind!' snapped Priam, obviously glad to let him down. 'Don't drag me into it. Honestly, bringing back blessed shrines that nobody wants. Go and bring Achilles' body, if you want to do something useful! Get back to the war!'

'And take that thing with you,' added Cassandra, with as much vehemence as she could muster, which was always considerable. But, as is well known, there are limits, and she had now reached them, as far as Paris was concerned.

'No, I say, really Cassandra, if you knew the weight of it! Can't I just move it to the side of the square, and leave it for the moment? As a sort of – well, as a monument, if you like?'

'A monument to what?' asked Cassandra, rudely, not letting the matter rest.

'Well, to my initiative, for instance. After all, it's the first sizeable trophy we've captured since the war started. It seems a pity not to make some use of it, don't you think?'

'And what sort of use would you suggest?'

'Well, *I* don't know, do I? Once we've examined it thoroughly, it will probably prove to have all sorts of uses.

'Yes, I'm quite sure it will; uses to the Greeks.'

'Now what on earth do you mean by that? The Greeks haven't got it anymore, have they? I have.'

She sneered, offensively: 'And why do you imagine they allowed you to capture it?'

This was going too far – even from a sister one has known from infancy.

'*Allowed* me to? Now, look here, Cassandra, I don't think you quite appreciate the sort of effort that went into –'

She ignored his local outburst. '*Where* did you find it?' she persevered, not letting up for an instant.

'Now, where do you think? Out there on the plain, for goodness sake.'

'Unguarded, I suppose?'

'Well as a matter of fact, yes. They're getting very careless these days.'

'I thought as much! Don't you see, you were *meant* to bring it into Troy?'

'No, I don't frankly. And furthermore...'

'I think I'm beginning to,' contributed Priam, gloomily.

Paris was now thoroughly on the defensive: 'Now, just what are you both getting at? Always have to try and spoil everything for me, don't you?'

Cassandra struck a dramatic pose, as though it had offended her in some way. 'This has broken my dream! The auguries were bad today, I awoke full of foreboding!'

'I never knew you when you didn't.'

'Paris,' said Priam, 'your sister is high priestess; let her speak.'

'Ah, very well, very well,' said Paris, yawning behind his chin-guard, 'what *was* this dream of yours, Cassandra?'

'Thank you! I dreamed that on the plain the Greeks had left a gift, and although *what* it was remained unclear, we brought it into Troy. Then in the night, from out its belly soldiers came, and fell upon us as we slept.'

'That's it?' asked Paris. 'Yes – well, I hardly think you need to interpret that one! Really, Cassandra, have you taken a good look at this gift – as you call it? Go on, take your time – examine it carefully – that's right. Now, just how many soldiers do you think are lurking in it? A regiment, perhaps? I hate to disappoint you, old thing, but you'd be lucky to prise even two small Spartans out of that.'

'Fools! Even one man could unbar the gates, and so admit an army! It's exactly the sort of scheme Odysseus would think of!'

'Then I hope I'm not being too practical for everybody,' returned Priam, reasonably, 'but why don't we open the thing and see?'

'Well, that's rather the trouble,' said Paris. 'There does seem to be a sort of door – but it won't open . . .'

'What did I tell you?' shrieked Cassandra, like an owl stuck in a chimney, 'It's locked from the inside!' And she beat her breast, in what must have been rather a painful way.

'Oh, *is* it?' Priam seized Paris's sword, 'Stand back! I have a short way with locks.' And he attacked the door of the TARDIS with ill-concealed malevolence. Not a dent or a blemish, however.

Paris swallowed a smug smile. 'Perhaps you'll believe me, next time? Cassandra, would you like to try?'

She rejected the offer with dignity. 'The thing need not be opened. Bring branches, fire and sacrificial oil! We will make of it an offering to the gods of Troy – and if there be someone within, so much the greater gift.'

While attendants, servitors and scullions scurried about to fetch the necessary, Paris had one final go at saving his hard-earned trophy.

'Now wait a moment all of you! Whatever it may be, the thing is mine – I found it! So leave it alone, can't you?'

But Priam's blood was really up now. He'd not only hurt his thumb on the door; but like Odysseus and Agamemnon before him, he resented being made a fool of, in front of the staff. 'Out of the way, boy! The thing must be destroyed before it harms us! Further.' he added, inspecting his damaged digit. Then, brandishing a burning branch, in a somewhat irresponsible manner, I thought, with so much sacrificial oil splashing about the place, he prepared to set fire to the TARDIS.

12

Small Prophet, Quick Return

From what I had heard the Doctor tell Odysseus, I suspected that the machine was pretty well indestructible anyway, but on the other hand, at the last count, one of our time travellers was missing. Or so Steven had told the Doctor; a young girl, if memory served – and naturally I didn't want her to be barbecued in her prime. So I mingled with the mob, and raised my voice among the general hubbub; and I raised it in quite a long speech too, because, if you notice, people are so used to short, snappy slogans on these occasions, that, in my experience, nobody pays a blind bit of attention to them. I mean 'Funeral pyre, out, out, out!' would simply fail to grip. So, clearing my throat, I said:

'Wait! It's not for me to tell you how to run things, of course, but before you actually initiate an irreversible conflagration, should we not pause to ascertain if such a gift would be *acceptable* to the gods? It may, of course, be exactly what they've always wanted, but, on the other hand, if it does harbour treachery, as Cassandra maintains, then might it not seem as if you're trying to shuffle it off on them? Because they'd hardly be likely to thank you for that, would they? Just an idea – thought I'd mention it.'

Not easy to say that sort of thing in a populist bellow, but I managed fairly well, I think, because it certainly held them for the moment. Paris tipped me the wink and gave me the thumbs up, and even Priam stopped in mid-ignition to consider my remarks.

'Yes, that *is* a point – we don't want a lot of offended gods to deal with, on top of everything else. Have a word with them, will you, Cassandra? Better to be on the safe side.'

She wasn't that pleased, but could hardly refuse, under the circumstances. Once more she struck that long-suffering attitude of hers. 'O, hear me, you Horses of the Heavens, who gallop with our destiny! If you would have us take this gift, then let us see a sign. Show us your will, I pray you, for we are merely mortal, and we need your guidance.'

Well, Vicki, as I had hoped, must have been glued attentively to the scanners watching the preparations for her incineration with some concern, because she very sensibly took Cassandra's harangue as a cue to come amongst us. She stepped out through the doors like a sylph from a sauna, and inquired politely, 'You need my guidance? I shall be prepared to help in any way I can.'

The effect was electric. Paris beamed and would certainly have twirled a moustache, if he'd had one about him. 'This is no Horse of Heaven,' he noticed approvingly.

'This is no Spartan soldier either,' Priam observed.

'Then *who* is she?' demanded Cassandra, obviously prepared to object, whoever she was.

'Ah, I'm no one of any importance,' said Vicki, decisively, 'but I do know a bit about the future, if that's what interests you?'

Well, of course it did – like anything! Except that Cassandra naturally felt that she should have a monopoly on that sort of thing, and bristled accordingly. 'How do you so? You are no Trojan goddess. You are some puny, pagan goddess of the Greeks.'

'Don't be silly – of course I'm not! I'm every bit as human as you are.'

'How comes it then, that you claim to know the future?'

'Oh, really, Cassandra,' said Paris, before Vicki could answer, 'you know you're always going on about it yourself.'

Having already bristled, Cassandra now bridled. '*I* am a priestess, skilled in augury!'

'Yes, yes, yes – all those dreary entrails, flights of birds and so on. We know. Well, perhaps this young lady's read the same ones?'

'Are you a priestess?' demanded Cassandra, prepared to make an issue of it.

'Not as far as I know. I mean, I never took any examinations, or anything.'

'Then how dare you practice prophecy?'

'Well, I haven't done yet, have I?' said Vicki, reasonably.

'You are some drab of Agamemnon's sent to spread dissension.'

It was Vicki's turn to bristle or bridle. She did both. 'What an idea! I'm nothing of the sort. Don't be coarse.'

'Of course she isn't,' said Paris 'I can tell.'

'Why, I've never even seen Agamemnon,' persisted Vicki, 'I wish I had, but I haven't.'

'Oh, you wouldn't like him at all,' said Paris, 'not at all your type.'

Priam coughed. 'Your judgement of young women, Paris, is notoriously unsound!'

Paris joined the bridling bristlers. 'Well, I don't care what anyone says – she's as innocent as she's pretty!'

'Then you'd better give her a golden apple, and get it over,' said Priam making an obscure classical reference. He turned to Vicki. 'Come here, child – I wish to question you.'

Cautiously, like a trout observing a label on a may-fly, Vicki left the shelter of the TARDIS, and approached the king.

'That's right. Now then, tell me – and you a Greek?'

'No,' said Vicki, 'I'm from the future. So you see, I don't *have* to prophesy – because, as far as I'm concerned the future has already happened.'

This was a facer, even for the wise old autocrat. 'Eh?' he inquired, 'I don't think I quite follow.'

'Of course, you don't,' snapped Cassandra, going in to bat again. 'She's trying to confuse you. Kill the girl,' she suggested spitefully, 'before she addles all our wits! If she isn't a priestess, then she's a sorceress, and deserves to die! There are standing orders to that effect.'

'Oh, don't be absurd, Cassandra – you're not to harm her,' said Paris, for the defence.

She turned on him like a viper – if that's the snake I mean. One of those frightfully quick ones, anyway – 'You purblind satyr. Why, you're half enchanted already. Get back to your Spartan adulteress, before you make a complete fool of yourself again. I tell you, she must die!'

'I do wish you'd both be quiet for a moment,' sighed Priam, 'Now, you mustn't be frightened, child; you shall die when I say so, and not a moment before.'

'That's very comforting,' said Vicki.

'Good girl! There – you see? Neither of you has any idea how to handle children. It only needs a little patience and understanding. Now, tell me first of all – what is your name?'

'Vicki,' said Vicki.

'Vicki?' he repeated doubtfully. 'That's an outlandish sort of name, isn't it?'

'A heathen sort of name if you ask me!' contributed his bouncing daughter.

'Nobody did ask you, Cassandra! Well, I really don't think we can call you Vicki – far too difficult to remember. No, we must think of another one for you. A Trojan type of name, that won't arouse comment. What about . . . let me see – what about Cressida? I had a cousin called Cressida once – on my father's side of the family. Always liked the sound of it. Would that suit you, do you think?'

'It's a very pretty name,' said Vicki.

'Very well, then – Cressida it shall be.'

'Thank you,' said Vicki, 'that's who I am, then.' And from that instant she was lost forever, and at last found her proper place in Time and History! For we are the prisoners of our names, more than ever we are of what we imagine to be our destinies. They shape our lives, and mould our personalities, until we fit them. We are only what our names tell us to be, and that is why they are so very important. And why, incidentally, the Doctor never revealed his own. It preserved his independence from Fate, and made him an unclassifiable enigma; which was an advantage in his line of work, as you will appreciate. I mean, supposing his real name had been ... but no – never mind! I digress again – and that's tactless of me, when Priam was still speaking.

'Now then, Cressida, you claim to come from the future?' She nodded modestly. 'So, presumably, you know everything that's going to happen?'

'Well, not absolutely everything, because, after all, I'm only quite young. There are lots of places and times I haven't been to yet.'

'Quite so. But on the other hand, I expect you know a good deal about this particular war we're having at the moment? Or you'd hardly be here, would you, now?'

She considered the question. 'Well to be honest, I only know what I've read. And I'm told a lot of that is only myth – nothing at all to do with what really happened.'

Confound the girl! My book is essentially true – although to be fair, I do embroider a bit here and there, for the sake of dramatic shape. Poetic licence, it's called – but then, as I say, I hadn't written it at the time; so I was as much in the dark as the rest of them.

'Never mind,' said Priam, the cunning old fox! 'Look, Cressida – come along into the palace, and you can, I'm sure, give me *some* sort of indication of what to expect, a general outline of Greek strategy, as it were; and in any case, I expect you could do with something to eat?'

'Thank you – yes, that would be very nice.'

'Yes indeed,' said Paris, 'I haven't had anything to eat since –'

Priam turned on him impatiently: 'You get back to the front. If you haven't killed Achilles by nightfall, I shall be very seriously displeased.'

'Oh, very well,' Paris agreed, gloomily, 'but I really don't see why Troilus shouldn't go? More his sort of thing.'

'Because you are now, Heaven help us all, my eldest son, and you must shoulder – I use the word loosely, of course – your responsibilities. And if, by any chance, Achilles should kill *you*, then Troilus will have *two* elder brothers to avenge – and will fight the better for it. Do you follow? That's the whole point!'

Paris saw it at once, of course, and didn't care for it. 'Well, I just wouldn't want to stand in his way, that's all.'

'Now, don't argue, Paris – just get out there!'

'Oh, all right. Goodbye Cressida. All being well, we shall meet this evening.'

'As soon as that?'

'Yes, we have to knock off as soon as the light goes, or you can't see the blood.'

'Oh, I see. Well, goodbye, Paris – and thank you for standing up for me.'

'Not at all, not at all,' said the unhappy prince, 'only too pleased.' And with a lack-lustre salute to whoever might be interested, he turned on his heel, and low-profiled back to the war.

'Now then,' said Priam, having thus inspired and invigorated his eldest, 'come along, Cressida – you and I must have a long talk. I've got a feeling you're going to bring us luck.'

'She will bring us nothing but doom, death and disaster,' remarked Cassandra, ever the optimist.

'Yes, yes, Cassandra – you *have* made your point. And your protest will be entered in the official records, so you've nothing to worry about. This way, my dear.'

Vicki hesitated. 'Are you quite sure? I dont want to upset anybody.'

'Oh, you mustn't worry about Cassandra – she always takes the gloomiest possible view of things. It's a form of insurance, I suppose, so that, if things *do* go wrong, she can always say – I told you so! I remember once...'

But what he remembered we shall never know, because at that point, he and Vicki disappeared into the palace – and I didn't think I should presume to follow them, on such a short acquaintance.

I was wondering what to do next, when Cassandra made up my mind for me. 'Hear me, you gods of Troy!' – and why she should have thought they were deaf I don't know – 'Strike with thy lightnings the fledgling upstart who seeks to usurp Cassandra, your true priestess! Or give me a sign, I pray you, that she is false – then will I strike the blow myself!'

Well she certainly looked capable of it, as she stalked back into the temple, slashing about her with a snake-skin whip, or some such; and for Vicki's sake, I hoped no sort of sign, as requested, was in the offing. But it didn't seem as if there'd be a lot I could do about it, even if there were. And, quite frankly, having had enough of Cassandra for one action-packed morning, I thought my best plan would be to stroll gently back to the Greek camp, and see how the Doctor was getting along with his war-plans.

Who knows – I might even be able to scrounge a bite of breakfast . . .

13

War Games Compulsory

I did, in fact, arrange to get a couple of rather bristly wild boar chops at the Greek commissariat, in exchange for a tune or two on my lyre – did I ever mention that I used to play a bit? And thus fortified, set out to find Odysseus' quarters – not easy in that ill-planned, haphazard straggle of a cantonment! – where I assumed he would have taken his prisoners. But being so obviously Greek myself, I was able to mingle at will amongst the lower ranks without exciting much curiosity; and eventually a hoplite of sorts suggested that I try down by the shore – apparently Odysseus kept himself apart from the other heroes whenever possible – and he pointed out where the Ithacan flotilla was drawn up on the sand, looking like so many stranded sea-monsters.

'You can usually find him there,' said my informant, 'when he isn't busy insulting his allies, or putting the fear of god into the rest of us with his crack-brained schemes.'

So I trudged seawards, and wandered moodily along the beach, aiming the occasional kick at a dead dog-fish, and wondering if I wouldn't be better employed getting the hell out of Asia Minor, and heading for the Hesperides, where I had a tentative concert engagement. In fact, I generally used to try and spend midsummer there when I could: cooler, you know, and very much nicer class of girl. So, thinking on these things, my steps were beginning to drag a bit; and I dare say that in another second or so I might well have given up the whole misguided project – when suddenly I heard my name mentioned. And that's something will always set a chap to eaves-dropping, no matter how many times he hears ill of himself.

So I peeked over the prow of the nearest long-ship; and yes – there were the Doctor and Steven, brows wrinkled and so on, poring over a lot of papers, and what looked like machine-drawings, spread out all over the – what do you call 'em? – thwarts, or something.

'No my boy,' the Doctor was saying, 'it couldn't possibly work in practice. It's obviously just something Homer thought up as a good dramatic device. I would never dream of doing it myself.'

Well, if he didn't dream of doing it soon, I'd never think it up at all. I could have told him that there and then!

That's one of the troubles with time-travel, you see. The Doctor was always so anxious not to alter the course of history by meddling, that he sometimes didn't realize history couldn't happen if he didn't give it a helping hand now and then. One sees the dangers, of course: get it wrong, and the whole future could be altered. And if you alter the future too much, you might very likely not get a chance to exist in it yourself, if you follow me? I suppose that's why, in later years, he always preferred to go forward rather than backwards in time; so that, whatever happened, he couldn't wipe himself clean off the slate by accident!

But the trick is: don't play the giddy-goat – just apply to the history books for instructions, and then get on with it. And since, apparently, I'd have written one myself before too long, all he had to do was what I told him. And I couldn't wait to hear what that was! I soon learnt, however; and, I must say, I was tempted to agree with him. The whole idea was preposterous!

'I don't see why,' argued Steven.

'Well, supposing we did build a great wooden horse, and fill the thing with soldiers, why on earth should the Trojans drag it into the city? They'd be far more likely to burn it where it stood – and a pretty lot of fools we should all look then! Especially the soldiers!' he added, after a pause.

'No, especially us,' Steven pointed out, 'after Odysseus got through with us! I'm afraid you're right, Doctor. And that being the case, you'd better hurry up and think of something else. We've only got forty-eight hours, remember!'

'Forty-two now, in point of fact,' said Odysseus pleasantly, climbing out of a sort of hatch-way, and swatting a wasp with a paint-brush. I suppose he'd been down in the bilges, caulking – or whatever it is you do in bilges. 'Haven't you thought of anything yet?'

'Nothing of any particular value,' admitted the Doctor, 'at least, nothing to bring about the fall of Troy. But I *have* thought of some conditions of my own.'

'That's very presumptious of you, I must say. I really don't see how you're going to enforce them. But you may as well tell me what they are, I suppose. After all, it's your time you're wasting – not mine.'

'It's simply this: if I'm to help you sack the city, then you must promise that Vicki will be spared.'

I was glad he'd remembered her at last. I was beginning to wonder. Odysseus looked puzzled. 'Vicki? What's that? And why should I spare it?'

'Oh, do pull yourself together, and pay attention!' said Steven – rather unwisely I thought. 'I told you about Vicki only this morning. And if they have taken the TARDIS into Troy, then she's probably still inside it.'

'I hope so, for her sake,' acknowledged Odysseus, 'because, if she left it, they'd assume she was one of *our* spies; and, in that case, I'd say she's probably past worrying about by now.'

'We can't be sure of that,' said the Doctor.

'Perhaps not – but I really don't see what you can expect me to do about it? You don't imagine, do you, that if and when we enter Troy, I shall have time to ask every young woman I see if she's a friend of yours, before I cut her throat? It just wouldn't be practical.'

'Then,' said Steven, 'let *me* go now, and try to get her out before you attack. After all, I'm no use to you here. The Doctor can manage very well without me.'

Odysseus rubbed his chin with the paint-brush – fortunately without noticing. Bluebeard, the bigamous pirate, to the life! 'I hope you don't think it's as easy to get into Troy as you suggest? If it were, I'd have done it myself years ago, and the war would be over by now.'

'I'm not proposing to *break* in – there are other ways.'

'Oh, are there indeed?' He yawned, inhaling a certain amount of paint. 'You must tell me about them sometime. At the moment I happen to be rather busy. Dam' barnacles get in everywhere,' he explained, preparing to descend to his bilges again.

'Listen a moment,' Steven persevered, 'it's quite simple. *You* can't afford to let yourself be taken prisoner – I can!'

Odysseus looked as near to pitying as he ever would. 'You really are anxious to die, aren't you? They'd take you for a spy, as we did.'

'Not if I were wearing uniform. I should be a prisoner of war.'

For a moment I was afraid Odysseus was going to laugh again. But wiser tonsils prevailed, and he spat out a gob of paint instead. He regarded it with astonishment – and then returned, a trifle subdued, to the subject under discussion.

'Hmm ... I'm not sure what they're doing with their prisoners of war at the moment. It *may* be just imprisonment, as you said. On the other hand, it may be hanging in chains for the vultures. Depends on how they feel at the time, I imagine. An unpredicatable lot, the Trojans.'

'I'm prepared to take the risk, if you're prepared to let me go.'

You could tell Odysseus was impressed, because he said so. 'You know, that's really very brave of you ... !'

'Then you'll help me?'

'I don't see why not. And, of course, if you can manage

to kill a couple of them before you let yourself be captured, we shall all be very grateful. Every little helps. And, as you say, you don't seem to be of any particular use here.'

'All right – I'll do my best. What about a uniform?'

'Can't help you there, I'm afraid – you'd look ridiculous in one of mine; altogether different fitting. Wait a minute – last week my friend Diomede died of his wounds on board – and they don't know he's dead – so you can take his identity as well as his armour. I'm sure he wouldn't mind, under the circumstances. You'll find his things up for'ard – and you're about his size, so, off you go.'

'Thank you, Odysseus – I'll try to be worthy of them.'

Tactful, I thought. A good lad.

'I'm sure you will be. I should have been quite distressed to have put you to death myself.' And he looked quite as if he meant it. So off Steven popped – and Odysseus turned to the Doctor: 'Well, now,' he said, 'after that, I hope *you're* not going to disappoint me?'

'I sincerely hope not. Tell me – have you thought of tunnelling?'

'It's been tried. The men won't work the hours. No, what we want is something revolutionary.'

'Dear me! I wonder – have you considered flying machines?'

Oydsseus raised an eyebrow, as with a winch. 'I can't say I have,' he admitted, 'tell me about them . . .'

'Flying machines, indeed! Enough of his nonsense!' I thought. 'It's time for my siesta.' For, in fact, the boar-chops were beginning to lie rather heavy – so I padded stealthily out of earshot and made a cautious way back to the plain, where there was a shady tree of which I had pleasant memories.

Just before I went to sleep, I remember thinking, 'Perhaps I'll give Hesperides a miss this year, after all. This is where the action's going to be, however eventually! And when it happens, it's sure to make good copy: The

72

Fall of Troy – an eye-witness account from your man in Scamander!'

Eye-witness? Well, Zeus be thanked, we don't know what to expect until it hits us!

Next time – if there is one – the Hesperides!

14

Single Combat

You will hardly believe this, but for the second time in twenty-four hours I was woken up by the sounds of battle – or by what I at first took to be the sounds of same – or by its vocal preliminaries, shall we say? Which, as we have seen, tend to be long and orotund, when compared to the usually brief and bloody sequel.

But, of course, I had forgotten that the war-like Paris was patrolling the plain, seeking whom he might devour – as per definite paternal instructions. So he was almost bound to make at least some sort of vengeful gesture, if he wanted his supper to be kept warm for him.

'Achilles!' he was calling quietly, 'Come out and fight, you jackal! Paris, the lion of Troy – and brother of Hector, if you remember? – seeks revenge!'

There was, of course, no reply; not even an echo from the ramparts, which weren't entirely sure they'd heard correctly.

He mopped his brow, and after a moment's thought enquired gently, 'Do you not dare to face me?'

And suddenly to the vast surprise of those present, there *was* an answer. '*I* dare to face you, Paris. Turn, and draw thy sword!' And, so help me, out of the bushes stepped Steven, looking every inch the long-awaited folk-hero, returned to save his people!

Well, he could have his people, and welcome, as far as Paris was concerned – he wasn't going to stand in anyone's way, that was quite obvious. But rallying swiftly, he put his finger on the flaw in Steven's suggestion. 'Ah,' he said, wagging a fore-finger, 'but then *you* are not Achilles, are you?'

'I am Diomede,' said Steven, 'friend of Odysseus,' he added, to establish his credentials.

Paris smiled with relief, and took the way out so kindly offered. 'Diomede, I do not seek *your* blood – I seek Achilles!'

He turned to continue the search; but Steven tapped him on the shoulder. 'And must Achilles, then, be roused, to undertake the death of such as you, adulterer?'

I must say he'd hit off the style to the very last alpha and delta – most impressive! You'd have thought he'd been talking like that ever since drama school. But Paris took the question as being rhetorical – and never mind the insult: 'I ... er ... I'm prepared to let that pass, for the moment. I assure you, I have no quarrel with you, Diomede!'

Not what Steven wanted at all. He resorted to out-dated patriotism. 'I am a Greek, and you a Trojan! Is *that* not quarrel enough?'

'Well, perhaps, in a general way,' conceded Paris, gracefully, 'but personally I think this whole thing has been carried a great deal too far. I mean, they should have let Menelaus and me settle it by the toss of a coin, like gentlemen ...'

This was becoming far more difficult than Steven had anticipated. He tried again. 'You are no gentleman, Paris! I've never thought so, and now I'm sure of it. Neither is Menelaus, come to that ...' he added, letting the style slip a little. Never mind – it worked: Paris stiffened indignantly.

'Now be very careful! You're taking everything far too seriously. Besides, are you aware you're speaking of one of your commanding officers? *And* one of my oldest friends, come to that? The Helen business was just a misunderstanding.'

'Which I now propose to resolve,' parried Steven, neatly. 'Draw thy sword, I say!'

To my astonishment, Paris began to do just that –
although, as if he'd read somewhere that slow motion
indicated menace. 'Very well,' he contrived to growl, 'but
you'll be sorry for this, I promise you!'

'That is a comfort, Trojan; I would not trust you to keep
a promise!'

There was no stopping the boy: but I thought he might
perhaps have overdone it now, because for the first time,
Paris looked angry. A chap can only take so much, after
all.

'Now there,' he said, 'I'm afraid you've gone very much
too far!' And suddenly he was no longer the fool and
coward he had looked and sounded; but a remarkably
efficient swordsman, out for the kill.

Fortunately for Steven he was quick on his feet, and
managed to dodge the first astonishing assault: but
obviously you can't keep that sort of thing up for ever, if
you haven't the remotest idea how to use a sword yourself.
So he did the only thing possible under the circumstances;
pretended to trip, fell on one knee, and – as Paris moved in
triumphantly for the death blow, said 'I yield!'

Paris was completely disconcerted. 'I beg your pardon?'
he enquired.

'I yield – I am your prisoner!' added Steven, clarifying
the position.

'Oh, but, now, look here – that simply is not done...
Surely you would rather die than be captured?'

'Well, yes, of course, as a rule I would,' admitted Steven;
'but little did I know when I challenged you, that you were
indeed the very lion of Troy! I am not worthy to be slain by
you. I should have listened to my friends...'

'Really?' enquired Paris, interested; 'Why, what do they
say?'

'That rather would they face Prince Hector – aye, and
Troilus, too – than mighty Paris. You are said to be
unconquerable.'

'Well, you really do astonish me! They don't say that in
Troy...'

76

'Then they must learn to! Oh, I could tell them tales about your valour which would make even grey-haired Priam blanch to hear them...'

Paris glowed. 'I say, could you really?'

'Aye – and will do! I pray Achilles may not meet you. Even now he prowls the plains – and what would happen to our cause, if *he* were vanquished?'

'Yes, I take your point,' said Paris, looking round apprehensively. 'But if I have a prisoner, I hardly think I can oblige him at the moment, can I? There *will* come a day of reckoning, no doubt; but not just now, obviously... On your feet, Diomede! If that's your name? Now will I drive you like a Graecian cur into the city! Farewell, Achilles! For today, Paris, Prince of Troy, has other business.'

Well, of course, like a fool, I wasn't going to miss a moment of this for anything; so off I trotted after them, back to the dear old impregnable fortress... just in time for a late tea, I hoped...

15

Speech! Speech!

Paris must have been getting used to seeing me about the place by now – after all, I'd played 'friendly voice in crowd' only that morning – *and* stopped his valued trophy getting scorched, into the bargain. So when he noticed me floundering after them through the common asphodel and other drought-resistant flora, he seemed quite pleased: called a halt and waited for me; then, when I caught up, offered to let me carry the prisoner, as a reward. I declined the honour, pleading a slipped discus; and he quite understood, being a martyr to that sort of thing himself.

So we entered the city in close formation: Paris at point, chin in air; Steven centre, head bowed in shame, as was only fitting; and yours truly bringing up the rear, the very picture of loyal retainer – and murmuring, 'Remember you are mortal, Commander', whenever the conqueror looked like overdoing the clasped hands above the head business. Which was pretty often, I must say: because apparently Steven was the only prisoner he'd ever captured – and naturally he wanted to make the most of it.

I didn't blame him in the least. A strange man, Paris; but one you couldn't help liking. Obviously he loathed the war, and everything about it; so it was easy to underestimate him, on that account. But for all that, he'd just proved that he could use a sword as devastatingly as the best of them, if there were really no alternative.

He just didn't fancy getting killed for no good reason, like Hector had been – and where's the harm in that, I ask?

78

I suppose when you come right down to it, the trouble was that he was an intellectual – which means, I take it, that you need to know the reason for everything, before not doing it. Well, even the best of military families is likely to throw up one of those every generation or so; and it probably explains why we got on so well – because I'm one myself in a quiet way, as you may have noticed.

Anyway, it was quite a decent little triumph, considering no one had had any time to prepare for it. A couple of trumpeters stopped larking about with their dice, as soon as they noticed us; and got fell in behind, as the expression is. After a brief discussion amongst themselves, they decided on a suitable programme; whereupon we were treated to a selection of gems from 'The Fair Maid of Troy' – and that soon brought the crowds out. Flags were waved in a desultory manner, and a startled cheer or two rang out; and as soon as he saw he'd got as much of their attention as was ever likely, Paris climbed on top of the TARDIS – which was still, thank Zeus, where he'd left it – and made a short speech.

'My friends,' he began, which was pushing it a bit, I thought, 'nobody can deny that total war is an unpleasant pursuit – especially when fought under the present conditions; against enemies who refuse to come out and be defeated like gentlemen!

'However, today I have met one honourable exception: my prisoner, the redoubtable and hitherto undefeated, deservedly popular hero, Diomede. Alone among the Greeks, he has dared to face me on the field of battle in single combat. So then; let's hear it for Diomede!'

After the very briefest respectful silence, he proceeded. 'Well, as you so rightly see, it did him no good; and that, in my opinion, makes his action all the more commendable, as he must have known from the outset how it would turn out! He had heard of my reputation, but nevertheless, he did not flinch from what he considered to be his duty. A strong man, you will notice – and as worthy an opponent as I am likely to find in a coon's age!

'And so I say this: it's a start! If only some of his companions are emboldened by his example to face me – or perhaps, rather, to face my brother, Troilus, who really ought to be given more of a chance – then the war can be brought to a swift and victorious end.

'So, in conclusion, let me remind you that we fight for the honour of the House of Priam, my well-known father; we fight for the honour of Troy itself; and lastly, we fight for the honour of Helen – as who has not, at some time or other?

'Thank you for your loyal attention, my friends – and may the Great Horse of Asia be over you always!'

At least that's what I *think* he said: and then sensing with his orator's instinct that he'd just about covered everything, he slid painfully off the TARDIS; and Steven and I followed him in to the palace, beneath a loyal hail of well-meant vegetable offerings.

No – public life will never be for me.

16

The Trojans at Home

I will say this for the Trojans: they did themselves uncommonly well when it came to the basic luxuries of life! It's odd, you know – one gets so used to the idea that we Greeks were the ones who rocked the cradle of civilization, and all the rest of it, that it comes as something of a shock to realize that the Trojans were way ahead of us when it came to gracious living. You won't find *that* in the history books, of course, because we wrote most of 'em ourselves; but I tell you, I was actually *there*, before the deluge, and I saw the whole thing: the cantilevered aqueducts, the under-floor heating, the splendid sanitary arrangements – the lot!

The architecture of the palace, for instance, was like nothing else I'd seen this side of Babylon – and I've been to most places, *and* beyond! Even from the outside, the building had been impressive; inside, it took your breath away – and a greater contrast to Agamemnon's tent could scarcely be imagined. *That* took your breath away for quite different reasons.

Marble featured prominently – and where they'd got it from I can't imagine! We Athenians have some in and around the Acropolis, of course – and long may it remain there – but then, we're sitting on top of the stuff; whereas Troy was built on oil-bearing shale, which is no use to anybody. So presumably Priam's ancestors must have hauled it with them from wherever they came from in the first place – which shows confidence, if nothing else! I

mean, you can just imagine it, can't you? 'We *are* going to
found a city, I tell you; so just get that Babylonian column
back on your shoulders, and look pleasant!' Otherwise
mutter and grumble, all the way to the coast – with the
Queen Mother saying she'd liked everything better where
it was . . .

All idle speculation, of course – but anyway, there it was
now; festooned here and there with silks and tapestries
showing Hercules and people about their vainglorious
business – and pictures of horses everywhere, with details
of their track records and pedigrees worked in gold thread
on a giant ivory stud-book. There was even a picture of
Helen's father – a swan, if you remember – which she must
have brought with her from Sparta. Probably snatched it
from her dressing table at the last minute, with Paris
teetering on the ladder with the luggage, and saying, 'For
god's sake, woman, we can't take *everything*!'

Anyway, most of the Royal Household had assembled
for refreshments in the dining-hall by the time we arrived;
and very interesting it was to see them all together, for
once. Most of the princes I didn't know, naturally; but I'm
not at all sure that Priam did either – there were so damn'
many of them! Deiphobus I'd heard of, and he must have
been about somewhere, but I couldn't place him.

That was the trouble, I suppose: the Trojans were just
one big, happy, well-off and privileged family – which is
decadent and reactionary. While the Greeks were a
quarrelsome bunch of unscrupulous riff-raff without two
morals to rub together – which is progressive; and meant
that they had to win in the end, because of the inevitable
tide of history, I'm told; although I don't see it myself.

Anyway, at least young Troilus was unmistakeable –
only about Vicki's age, I would say, and absolutely the god
Apollo to the life. Or possibly Hermes? One of those
devilish good-looking ones, who zip about Olympus, you
know.

And the nice thing was, he seemed to be completely
unaware of it – just a pleasant, unspoilt, all-Trojan boy;

with promise of being every bit as much a force to be reckoned with as his brother Hector – if he managed to live long enough, that is. And I wouldn't have banked on that at the time, knowing as I did what the Doctor and Odysseus were cooking up for them beyond the city walls.

There were only three ladies present: and one of them was Vicki – or Cressida, as I suppose I should call her now – and she was obviously enjoying herself no end. She was sitting in the place of honour, at Priam's right hand – dressed like a princess; and looking absolutely radiant, as princesses always do. My word – she had done well for herself since this morning, and no mistake! A complete transformation! No longer the lovable young tom-boy space-urchin; but a raving beauty, secure in the knowledge of her newly discovered devastating powers, which at the moment she was turning full blast on poor young Troilus, who sat at her feet looking as if he didn't know his heart from tea-time – he was eating it out, anyway; that much was quite clear!

'Well, good luck to them both,' I thought; 'it had to happen sometime – and the sooner the better, the way things are!'

This view was obviously not favoured by the second lady present, whom we have met before. Cassandra, seething with ill-concealed malice, was toying absent-mindedly with a gem-encrusted goblet, as if trying to remember the exact formula for turning young lovers into frogs. What an unpleasant woman, to be sure!

But the third of the trio couldn't have cared less what was going on as long as the rest of the men gave her their full and undivided attention. 'What's one adolescent princeling more or less?' Helen seemed to be thinking; 'there's bound to be plenty more along in a moment.'

I suppose I should try to describe her – although it isn't easy. Other – even, arguably better writers than I, have tried; and made a thoroughly inadequate mess of it. And I think I know the reason – or one of the reasons, anyway.

Helen, you see, was one of those women who are not

only all things to all men; but who are different for each of those men – that's the point.

Do this now – as they say when they're trying to sell you something: write down your own ideal of absolutely perfect, quintessential feminine beauty – why should I do all the work? – and that would be Helen – for *you*. But for you, alone! Because I'll bet if you showed that description of yours to someone else who'd seen or imagined her, he'd proceed to describe someone quite different – his own ideal, you see?

Why, even her hair seemed to change colour while you were actually looking at her: and her figure seemed to flow and mould itself from one sensuous shape to another, like an amoeba looking for a meal! It was quite uncanny. Was she tall or short, plump and voluptuous, or slim and athletic? Impossible to say. All I do know, is that *whatever* she looked like in fact, the image of what you *thought* she was would be what you'd been looking for all your life; and what you wanted right now, thank you very much! And furthermore, what you wanted right now, would be what you'd always remember as long as you lived. *I've* never forgotten her, and I'm going on eighty – but damned if to this day I can tell you why. Just one of those things.

As to her voice . . . well, to be honest, I don't recall her actually saying anything – but then, with her looks, whatever they were, she didn't need to. Oh, no doubt she made the odd remark, like 'Pass the Oriental spices, would you?' – but if so, I don't remember. No – a neat trick she had, and no mistake!

Menelaus must have been mad to let her go; but Paris would have been mad not to have taken her; and that of course, was the insoluble root of the whole stupid trouble. I'd have died for her, myself – and very nearly did, come to that.

Still, I don't know . . . it would have been very tiring living with Helen; with everyone from milkman to tax-inspector trying to get her alone for a moment; so perhaps I'm well out of it? But you can't help thinking – even now

– can you? Well, at any rate. I can't!

But enough of maudlin fantasy and vain regrets. I have a story to tell, and must get on with it . . .

17

Cassandra Claims a Kill

In spite of Paris understandably wanting to make the big entrance, nobody seemed to notice us much at first. Troilus, you see, was looking at his Cressida; Cassandra was glaring at the pair of them; and all the others were looking at Helen; who, in turn, was affectionately contemplating her reflection in a bowl of soup.

So for a while we hovered in the offing; while Priam did his best to ply Cressida with shrewd questions about the future. And he wasn't getting very far, because she kept changing the subject. No fool, that girl! In fact, as far as questions were concerned, she was making most of the running.

'How on earth,' she asked, helping herself to another slice of breast of peacock, 'do you manage to live like this, when you're under seige?'

'Well,' said Priam, modestly, 'my nephew, Aeneas, brings us a little something from time to time. He's in charge of our mobile force, d'you see? Raids the Greeks supply lines with his cavalry. They think it's barbarian bandits,' he chuckled; 'but in fact, they do contrive to keep us in a certain style.'

As a grand inquisitor, he'd have been nowhere! All this would have been nuts and wine to Agamemnon, I couldn't help thinking.

'I didn't know such a thing as cavalry existed yet,' she said, reaching for the lotus sauce with a tablespoon. Still a child in many ways, in spite of everything.

'Oh, bless my soul, yes,' said Priam, ignoring the gaffe, 'we're all horsemen at heart, you know. The Greeks laugh at us for our horse-gods: but I sometimes think that if we'd kept all our strength in cavalry, we'd have done far better. Swept 'em back into the sea where they belong, years ago. No, to be honest, I'm afraid we'ye gone rather soft in here, behind the walls. There's nothing like security, Cressida, to sap the initiative – so think of that, before you go looking for it. Take my advice,' he said, glaring at Troilus, 'and before you think of settling down, get yourself a horse. A horse is a fine animal; a good horse will carry the day every time. The very last word in warfare, a horse is! That's why a Trojan will do anything for a horse!'

This, one might have thought, could well have exhausted the subject of horses; but Cressida paused with a forkful of imported Herperidean asparagus half-way to her lips. 'It's funny you should say that about horses...' she reflected.

'Funny? Why, what do you mean?' said Priam, prepared to be offended. 'What's funny about a horse?'

'Oh, nothing really... just reminded me of a story I read, a long time ago...'

The fork continued its interrupted journey, and Priam watched it with interest.

'A story about this war, by any chance?'

'Well, yes – but nothing of any importance, I'm sure. It's just a silly legend...'

'What sort of silly legend? Now look here, young Cressida, I'm relying on you to tell us everything you know, before you eat yourself to – I mean, if you really do come from the future, the smallest detail may be important!'

'I suppose it may,' acknowledged Vicki. 'Troilus, you're not eating anything. Aren't you hungry?'

Troilus blushed, and admitted to having rather lost his appetite just lately.

'But you must have something, you know, or you won't keep your strength up.'

What a ridiculous remark! The boy was a rippling mass of muscle!

'Go on, you must force yourself,' she persevered, offering him her plate...

Greater love et cetera... But Priam interrupted. 'Never mind Troilus and his anaemia! I want to hear this legend about a horse. I like a good horse story,' he explained unnecessarily.

'Oh, well,' she began; 'it's just that the Greeks –'

But at this moment Paris coughed, and stepped forward to take his share of delayed limelight. On such trivial circumstances rest the destinies of nations!

'Father,' he announced, 'I've captured a Greek!' And like Achilles, not so many hours ago, he looked in vain for popular acclamation. It seemed to be the dawning of the age of the anti-hero. No one seemed in the least interested or impressed.

In fact, quite the contrary. 'Confound you, Paris!' exclaimed Priam. 'When will you learn not to come bursting in here when I'm busy?' The two faithful trumpeters took the hint, paused in mid-fanfare, and sidled back where they came from.

'I'm sorry, father, I just thought you might want to question him...'

'Well, so I may, in due course, but – Great Heavens – that isn't *him* is it? What in Hades do you want to bring him into the banquetting hall for? Can't you see we're in the middle of dinner? Bringing in rotten prisoners, scattering mud and blood everywhere! Get him out of here!'

Paris took a deep breath, and squared, approximately, his shoulders: 'He is *not* in the least rotten – he is an officer, and perfectly clean. In fact, he's a hero, and one of their very best, so I think you should speak to the man, especially as he's come all this way. Step forward, Diomede!'

As Steven obeyed, Cressida looked reluctantly away from Troilus for one moment – and choked over an olive the next. 'Steven,' she squeaked; 'What on earth are you doing here – dressed like that?'

Steven cast his eyes to heaven, as they say. 'Please be quiet, Vicki,' he hissed through the gritted teeth he kept at the corner of his mouth. But too late, of course: the damage was done.

Priam recoiled – the picture of a king who's been put upon. '*What* was that he called her?' he enquired icily.

Cassandra now took centre-stage; the picture of a prophetess who'd told everyone as much. 'You heard, didn't you?' she asked, superfluously. 'That was the name she called herself when we found her! *And* she recognized him, too! And since he's a Greek, what more proof do you want that she's a spy? Kill her! Kill both of them! Kill! Kill! Kill!'

Well, that seemed to sum up the general feeling of the meeting; and as Vicki ran idiotically to Steven for protection, instead of leaving things to Troilus and Paris to sort out, I sidled inconspicuously after the trumpeters. There didn't seem to be anything further I could usefully do; but I thought it might be a good idea at this point, to let the Doctor know what was going on. I wanted to meet him anyway – and this seemed like the perfect opportunity.

18

The Ultimate Weapon

I was getting to know my way back and forth across the
plain rather well by now; and keeping a weather-eye open,
of course, for embattled heroes blaring iambics at each
other, it didn't take me too long to arrive back at Odysseus'
ship. Oh, the merest hour, I should think. After all,
Scamander wasn't a big plain as plains go – not your
steppes of Asia by any means: and the only problem was,
you had to keep fording that little river, which wandered
about all over the place like a brook intoxicated. The
Meander, I remember it was called; and it, well, it
meandered to coin a phrase.

Anyway, I arrived, as I say, rather damp; but most
fortunately, as it seemed at the time, just as Odysseus had
dropped in for a routine check on the Doctor's progress;
and I must say, as far as I could see from my hiding place in
a thicket of sea-holly, he didn't seem to have made much.
Nevertheless . . .

'I think this may interest you,' said the Doctor, without
much confidence. He produced an armful of drawings,
and spread them out on the hatch way in the evening sun.
'You were asking me about flying machines, I believe?'

'No, I wasn't – you were telling me about them. Well?'
rumbled Odysseus, discouragingly.

'Well, this is one of them . . .' And to my horrified
amazement, he had the gall to produce a paper dart from
amongst the documents, and fling it over the side of the
boat; where it nose-dived into a decomposing starfish.

Odysseus noted the fact without enthusiasm. 'What did you say it was?' he enquired – with admirable self control, I thought.

'A flying machine,' repeated the Doctor, proudly.

'It looks more like a parchment dart, to me. My son, Telemachus, used to make them to annoy his tutors. So did I, come to that!'

'Oh, did you, indeed?' said the Doctor, somewhat taken aback.

'Yes. And rather better ones, if you must know.'

But the Doctor was nothing if not resilient. 'Excellent,' he cried; 'Capital! If you're already familiar with the basic principles, it makes it very much easier to explain. That dart is merely the prototype of a very simple aerial conveyance!'

'What are you talking about now?'

'Don't you see, it would be possible to build a very much larger one, capable of carrying a man?'

'And what earthly good would that do?'

'Think, my dear Odysseus: a whole fleet of them could carry a company of your men over the walls, and into Troy!'

'Oh could they now? And how would we get them into the air?'

'Catapults!' said the Doctor, producing his fatuous master-stroke. 'Ping!' he illustrated.

'I beg your pardon?'

'Catapults. I thought you'd have heard of them.'

'No, I can't say I have. Catapults, d'you say? Sounds like a rather vulgar barbarian oath to me. Yes, I must try it out on Agamemnon – Catapults to you, my lord! And very many of them! Yes ...'

The Doctor grew impatient: 'Nonsense, Odysseus! A catapult is ... well, look here, you could easily make one out of strips of ox-hide. I've made a drawing of one. First, you twist the strips together – so. Then you fasten the two ends securely. Next, you take up the slack in the middle, and you stretch it like a bow string.'

'Go on – what do I do then. Use it as a hammock?'

'Nothing of the sort! You pour water over it, and leave it to dry in the sun. Now, tell me Odysseus; what happens then, eh?'

'It begins to smell, I should think.'

'Never mind that, for the moment. It also shrinks, doesn't it? Thereby producing the most colossal tension between the two points here. So, now you place your flying-machine at the point of maximum strain . . . C.'

'Like an arrow in a bow?'

'Precisely! And then, you let go!'

'Always as well to remember to do that!'

'And Eureka! It flies up into the air, with a soldier clinging to its back – and it glides, following a curvilinear trajectory, over the wall, and into the very heart of Troy! Nothing could be simpler!'

A passing seagull made a harsh comment, as Odysseus considered the matter 'I see . . .' he said at length; 'Well, for your information, Doctor, here's one soldier who's doing nothing of the sort!'

The Doctor looked caring and compassionate: he had every sympathy with human frailty, and said so. 'Well, perhaps Agamemnon, then – if you're afraid?'

'Now *that* might be quite an idea!' mused Odysseus, cheering up somewhat. 'But no – he wouldn't go along with it . . .'

'Whyever not? It would be a privilege.'

'I know – but he wouldn't see it that way. Fellows a fool! No – we'll have to think of someone else.'

'Well, anyone would do: a child could operate it!'

'Really? Or an old man?'

'Oh yes, of course he could. Old Nestor would do admirably.'

'I wasn't thinking of Nestor!'

'You weren't?'

'No. Tell me, Doctor – how would you feel about being the first man to fly?'

The Doctor's brain raced in ever-diminishing circles. I

could tell by his ears which went puce.

'Well,' he said, 'I should be extremely honoured, of course.'

'I hoped you might be. You deserve it, after all the hard work you've put in.'

'Yes. But, dear me – there's a problem.'

'Good thing you thought of it in time. What is it?'

'The machine won't work!'

'Are you sure?'

'Positive. Yes, look here – I seem to have made a mistake in my calculations. The weight-volume ratio's all wrong, do you see? Silly of me!'

'Very.'

'No, we'll just have to face it, I'm afraid: man was never meant to fly!'

'Oh, I don't know about that. I mean, if your machine won't work, you'll just have to fly without it, won't you?'

'What . . . what do you mean?'

'Well, surely the catapult *will* work all right. I think that's a *very* good idea of yours – and it seems such a pity to waste it, that I propose to fire you over the walls of Troy. Then you can help *them* for a change. That'll teach 'em!'

'But I should be killed!'

'You must do as you think best. But since you have failed me, you are now expendable.'

'Wait! I haven't failed you yet!'

'You mean, there's *more*?'

'Oh, a very great deal! Yes, I've just had a far better idea!'

'Nothing like the prospect of death to concentrate the mind, is there? Go on!'

The Doctor took a deep breath, and sentenced the world to Greek civilization.

'What would you say to a horse?' he asked.

'Is it a riddle?'

'No, no – of course not! I mean, a huge wooden horse – Oh, about forty feet high, I should think. Look. I'll do you a drawing.'

'Don't bother – I know perfectly well what a horse looks

93

like.'

'Good. Then that's the first half of the battle.'

'I can't wait for the second. What on earth are you rambling on about now?'

'I'm trying to tell you, aren't I? Listen – you make the body of the horse hollow; then you fill it with your picked warriors; and you leave it on the plain for the Trojans to capture! How about that?'

'It would be one way of solving our food shortage, I suppose. Got any more ideas?'

'I do wish you'd pay attention! Can't you see – they'll drag it into the city?'

'It's my belief you're demented! Why on earth would they do a silly thing like that?'

'Because,' said the Doctor triumphantly, 'they'll think it's the Great Horse of Asia, come down to save them!'

There was a long pause.

'And just how would they expect it to do that?' asked Odysseus, having looked at the plan from every angle.

'By frightening away the Greek army. Because that's what it would seem to have done, wouldn't it? Everyone of you not required for horse-construction duty, would sail away over the horizon.'

'And only come back once the horse is inside the gates?'

'Precisely! Splendid! I knew you'd see it! Well, how does it strike you?' asked the Doctor, excited as if he'd thought of it himself. What we writers really need is absolutely water-tight copyright laws; but I don't suppose we'll ever get 'em.

'I must think it over,' said Odysseus, cautiously. 'At least, I don't think its ever been done before,' he admitted. 'On the other hand, that might be against it, in certain quarters... Tell you what, give me half an hour to work out a few details.'

'To quantify the project,' murmured the Doctor, beaming like Archimedes on a good day.

'If you prefer it. And if I can't find a flaw, we'll ask Agamemnon over for a drink, and put it to him.'

Well, of course, I couldn't wait half an hour to tell the Doctor the bad news about Steven and Vicki; because, if they weren't already dead, they were bound to be in prison, waiting to be executed by the due process of law; so there wouldn't be all that long for him to hang about congratulating himself, if he was going to get them out of it: certainly not long enough for him to build a damn' great wooden horse, I wouldn't have thought.

The snag was that Odysseus showed no signs of being about to retire to his cabin to do his thinking, no, he kept pacing the deck, growling to himself, and occasionally giving one of those great diabolical laughs of his. So there was obviously going to be no chance of getting the Doctor alone for a moment.

But Odysseus did seem to be in a good enough mood, judging by the sound effects: so I thought I'd better risk it, and gamble on the possibility of his not killing me before good faith could be established.

I therefore stepped confidently out of the shadows, and – probably the bravest thing I've ever done – hopped buoyantly over the gunnels to deliver my message.

'Doctor,' I said, 'you don't know me, but I assure you I'm a friend: and I have to tell you that Steven and Vicki have both been captured, and sentenced to death by the Trojans. Mind you the Trojans don't seem to be at all bad chaps on the whole; and I'm sure a word in the right quarter, possibly from you, Lord Odysseus – would resolve the matter of their identity in no time. But *something's* got to be done – because it's that Cassandra, you see? She's the one who wants them to die; for various reasons which I won't bother you with now, because there isn't a lot of time.'

Well, I thought that wrapped the whole thing up rather neatly, considering I hadn't done a lot of this exhausted messenger gasping out the tidings business before. I had considered clutching one of them by the arm for support; but decided against it, as being a touch too melodramatic. No – I was relying on the element of surprise, you see; the theory being that if you don't give anyone else a chance to say anything, there's not a lot they can do about it till you've finished. I've often noticed that chaps don't seem able to kill other chaps to their faces, until they've told them that that's what they're going to do. A sort of convention, I suppose it is.

And, do you know, it more or less worked? Because Odysseus didn't actually kill me: he put out my right eye with a marlin-spike, instead! And then he laughed – just to show that everything was all right, really.

'Sorry,' he said, 'my hand slipped. So you like the Trojans, do you? Well now, my little Cyclops, you'll just have to learn to take a more one-sided view of things, won't you?'

And then, I'm afraid, I fainted.

19

A Council of War

Of course, after the lapse of forty-odd years, I can afford to take a rather less jaundiced view of the matter than I did at the time. Now, I suppose I must admit that the whole thing was largely my own fault: I should never have said that I quite liked the Trojans! Simply asking for it. Because one of the traditions of war is that you have to believe the enemy are fiends incarnate. And anyone who takes the opposite view is not only on their side, but a bounder and a cad into the bargain. In fact, why Odysseus didn't kill me I shall never know: but perhaps he thought he had. After all, that sort of wound can often be fatal – especially when delivered without proper surgical care.

I like to think that the Doctor made some sort of protest, however ineffectual; and no doubt he did. But there wasn't a lot he could actually *do*, without getting the chop himself. Quite! Yes, I can understand that – *now*. But at the time I was ... well, sour, about the whole episode.

'That's what you get for trying to do someone a good turn!' I thought, as I came to, some hours later. I was lying in the scuppers, where Odysseus had obviously kicked me, not wanting bleeding corpses cluttering up the deck. To add to my pleasure, I was covered in fish-scales and crabs' legs, and other marine bric-à-brac of a more or less noisome nature; and I suppose I should mention in passing that I was in the most excruciating pain I had ever known – or had believed was generally available outside the nethermost circle of Hades! No point in going on about it: but I tell you, I wanted to die, and was very sorry to find I hadn't. *That's* what it was like – so I'll trouble you to bear the fact in mind, if you think I'm being altogether too flippant. In any case, as I say, it was all a very long time ago.

But to resume: it was dark by now, Zeus be praised; except where a lantern illuminated the Doctor's designing board, and a selection of brooding evil-looking faces. Because Odysseus had obviously sent out the formal invitations as arranged; and Agamemnon and Menelaus were now among those present. A couple of death's head moths were fooling about in the lamp-light, I remember. All very well for them, I thought – but somehow ominous, all the same. Not that I go much on signs and portents as a rule – but you know what I mean.

The genial host was excited as a schoolboy, and busy explaining the whole horrendous scheme to his dubious guests.

'I tell you, it's revolutionary,' he was saying, 'war will never be the same again!'

'Show them the working-drawings, Doctor. There! What do you make of that?'

Understandably, no one seemed very impressed at the outset – and you couldn't blame them. Surprisingly, Menelaus was the first to venture a diagnosis.

'It's a horse,' he said, 'isn't it?'

'Well done, Menelaus,' said Odysseus, patronisingly. 'Now, come on – what *sort* of a horse?'

Menelaus tried again: 'A *big* horse?'

'Precisely. A *very* big horse. A horse at least forty feet high!'

'But,' objected Menelaus, 'they don't grow that big – do they? I mean, not even that Great Horse of Asia the Trojans worship.'

'Ah, *now* you're beginning to get the point! They *don't* grow that big. The Great Horse of Asia doesn't exist. That's why we're going to build one for them – as a sort of present!'

98

'Go on,' said Agamemnon, his slow brain stirring in its sleep.

The Doctor took over the sparkling exposition: 'We build it of wood, and we build it hollow. And what's more we build it as quickly as possible, so as to rescue my friends. And then we fill it with a picked team of your best warriors.'

'I'm with you so far. What next?'

'Why, the rest of you take the fleet, and you sail away!'

Menelaus lit up a bit at that. 'Marvellous!' he said. 'A first rate idea! Oh, yes – I like it very much!'

'And then, after dark, you sail back again.'

Menelaus subsided. 'Why is there always a catch?' he grumbled. 'No, I'm afraid I've gone off it now!' But nobody cared what Menelaus thought.

'Now,' said Odysseus, 'we come to the difficult bit. Because someone has to winkle Achilles out of his tent for long enough for him to take his Myrmidons, and hide out there in the plain. As a covering force,' he explained patiently, before anyone could ask him why.

'But I thought you said that the best warriors were going to be inside the horse?' objected Agamemnon, rooting about in his beard, where something had come to his attention.

'So they will be,' agreed Odysseus; 'I shall be there with my Ithacans. Oh, yes, *and* the Doctor, of course.'

The Doctor leaped like a gaffed salmon. 'That wasn't part of the plan!' he objected.

'It is now. I've just thought of it. Don't you want to be on hand, to rescue your friends?'

'Yes, of course. But can't I join you later? I'm afraid I should only be in the way...'

'You'd better not be, that's all. No, Doctor, I prefer to keep my eye on you. And then the rest is up to the Trojans. They see we've all gone home, or so they think; and naturally assume it's the Great Horse which has driven us away. So they dance around it like maniacs; cover it with garlands, I should think; and then they drag it into the city!'

'Are you sure they do?' enquired Agamemnon, not unreasonably. 'Suppose they set fire to it? In my experience, you never know *what* those damn' fellows are going to do . . .'

'That is a calculated risk,' said the Doctor, 'but I've given the matter some thought, and they'd hardly destroy one of their own gods, would they?'

'All right – but once they've got the horse inside, won't they close the gates again?'

'Oh, dear,' sighed Odysseus. 'Yes, Agamemnon, old war lord, of course they will. But during the night, my men will leave the horse and open them again, won't they? Thus, if you follow me closely, letting the rest of you in. Nothing could be simpler,' he concluded triumphantly, rolling up the battle plan.

Well, of course it couldn't: provided, that is, the Trojans were working from the same script! But I'd heard enough to be going on with: and while they were all busy, slapping each other on the back, and saying how clever they were, I dragged my bleeding remains over the bulwarks; and, sobbing and stumbling, I set out for Troy once more.

20

Paris Stands on Ceremony

A silly thing to do, you may think – but remember, I wasn't reasoning too clearly at that time: and the only thought in my throbbing head was that if Vicki and Steven had to wait for the doctor to get his ridiculous horse built before they were rescued, what was left of them might not be worth the effort. So I trudged back across that damn' plain – keeping a wary look-out, with my remaining eye, for the beasts of the field; because a jackal or so had picked up my blood-trail, and were following along, nudging each other and chuckling in anticipation. Well, one can cope with jackals – but one doesn't want lions, or things of that nature; and in those days there were a good few of them about. So, as I say, I was careful.

And just as well, too – because I nearly trod on my old friend Paris, who was sensibly taking a little time out from war, under a hibiscus bush.

'Hello, again,' he said, 'so there you are. I was wondering where you'd got to. What on earth's that on your face?'

I told him it was probably the remains of my eye – and explained as much of the circumstances as seemed advizable, without mentioning the Doctor, of course. He was most sympathetic; and, as far as he could without proper facilities, helped me to clean up the mess. As I say, he was a decent enough chap at heart – I doubt if his sister would have done as much; probably made some crack about blind Fate, or something equally tactless.

But even so, I wasn't going to tell him about the Trojan horse – not while it remained the only chance of getting the Doctor's friends back – and as he babbled resentfully away about how he'd always wanted to be a shepherd, and how difficult his father could sometimes be, I managed to gather just what had happened after I left the royal apartments. Apparently Steven and Vicki hadn't been killed outright; so that was encouraging for them.

Now, remember that what follows is the story as I had it from Paris, out there on the plain that night, with the jackals yapping about us, and birds of ill-omen shouting the odds – and by Zeus, I wish I'd paid more attention to them! – so you mustn't be surprised if he comes out of it rather well.

Cassandra, you will recall, had just launched one of her well-known and popular diatribes culminating in a death-wish; at which point I had held it tactful to withdraw my brooding presence from the proceedings. But Paris, if we are to believe him, stepped forward as angrily and boldly as a boa-constrictor about to be robbed of its breakfast.

'Since when have you given orders to the military, Cassandra? Guards – put up your weapons! I am in command here!'

'Of everything but your senses, it seems,' she sneered.

'It pleases you to make frivolous observations? So be it. Nevertheless, since Hector's death, I am officer commanding all Trojan forces in the Middle East; and I will not tolerate interference from a fortune-teller of notorious unreliability!'

That shook her. 'How dare you? I am high-priestess of Troy!'

Well, she was, of course; but apparently nothing could stop Paris now.

'Then get back to your temple, before you give us all galloping religious mania! I really cannot face another of your tedious tirades at the moment!'

The church's one foundation rocked on its heels.

'Father,' she appealed, 'do you hear him?'

Priam smiled into his napkin: 'Yes, it's most refreshing. Perhaps there is a man lurking behind that flaccid façade, after all.'

Having got so far without being struck from the records, Paris went further. 'And I would be obliged, father, if you would refrain from patronizing me in front of the prisoner!'

Helen, of course, didn't say anything, but her looks spoke slender volumes. You could tell she was impressed. Priam, on the other hand, wasn't. 'The prisoner? Yes, of course, that's it! One pathetic prisoner, and he thinks he's Hercules, already! Success has gone to his head!'

'Before you start sneering at the prisoner, you'd better hear who he is. This is Diomede! *Steven* Diomede, possibly – but a lot of us have damn' silly first names. And if you'll take the trouble to look in the Greek Army Lists, you'll discover he's quite a catch!'

Flattered, Steven decided to take a hand. 'Which none but you could have caught, O lion of Troy!' he said humbly.

This went down like ipecacuanha after sago! The audience choked as one.

'Eh?' enquired Priam, rotating a finger in his ear.

'What was that?' demanded Cassandra, rotating in her turn, but through ninety degrees.

'Yes, I thought you might be surprised,' said Paris. 'Want to tell them about our little spot of sabre-rattling, Diomede?'

Steven delivered a modified digest of their late encounter. 'We fought; I was defeated; I am not ashamed. There is none in all our ranks who could stand against the wrath of Paris, when he seeks revenge!'

'You see?' Paris appealed to the company at large. 'I am treated with more respect by the enemy than by my own family!'

'Perhaps they don't know you as well as we do,' explained Cassandra, helpfully.

103

'On the other hand, perhaps they know me rather better,' said Paris, imperturbably, knocking back a nectar in one, 'and perhaps the time has come, dear sister, to revise your opinions?'

'I am perfectly familiar with my opinions, thank you; and revision will not be necessary. And the first of them is that Cressida and Diomede have clearly met before: so how do you explain that?'

'My dear old entrail-watcher, how in Hades should I know? But since Cressida says she pops about in Time as her whimsy wafts her, I should think she's met lots of people, haven't you, Cressida?'

'That's right,' said Vicki, rising to the occasion, 'of course, I have. Surely, Diomede, it was at the Olympic Games, last year? You won the Pentathlon, didn't you?'

'So I did – I mean, so it was,' said Steven, 'and then we all went on to Diana's Grove, afterwards; and you told everybody's fortune, I remember. What a night that was! All came true, too! Goodness knows how you did it.'

'Just a knack!' said Vicki, modestly.

'Sorcery!' snarled Cassandra, reverting to her main thesis.

'Quite so,' said Priam. 'Well, whether it's sorcery, or palmistry, or tea-leaves, or just time-travelling, or whatever it is, we could use some of it right now. So, if you are who you say you are, Cressida, now's your chance to prove it: you must either give me information which will lead us to a speedy victory – or, if you prefer it, you can use your supernatural powers to turn the tide of battle in our favour. It's entirely up to you.'

'I'll do what I can, of course,' said Vicki, 'but you must promise not to harm Diomede.'

'I suppose that could be arranged – or, at any rate, postponed. Tell you what I'll do: I'll give you a whole day to come up with something. How about that?'

'Well I'll try,' said Vicki, doubtfully, 'but it's not very long. What happens if I can't?'

Cassandra knew the answer to that one. 'You will be

burnt, as a sorceress, a false prophet, and a spy!'

'Well, as one of them, anyway,' conceded Priam, reasonably, 'we don't want to overdo things. And now, unless Paris has any objections, of course, I think you should both be taken away!'

'No, I must say, I think that's very fair,' said Paris, honour being satisfied. 'I'm sure you'll find the dungeons quite comfortable, Diomede. I often spend a quiet hour or two down there myself, when I want to get away from things. Yes, Cressida – you're bound to find them the perfect place for thinking.'

So off they were taken to the dungeons. And there, presumably, they still were.

21

Dungeon Party

Well, I was pleased to know they were still alive, of course; but I can't say I liked the way things were shaping one little bit. You see, even if it were possible to get word through to Vicki that the Doctor's fortunes were riding on a horse, so to speak – thus enabling her to warn Priam, and do herself a bit of good thereby, think what *that* would do to the Doctor! He was going to be inside the infernal machine, if you remember; so that if the Trojans decided to burn it – whoops! And if they just decided to leave the thing where it was, looking foolish, or dance round it jeering, then Odysseus was going to be extremely cross at the farcical failure of the plan; and I had every reason to know what he was like in that mood! I wouldn't wish to be cooped up with him in a horse's stomach under those circumstances, thank you! So either way the Doctor was for it, it seemed to me.

But if I didn't do *anything*, then the first thing the Trojans would do, once they realized they'd been tricked, would be to get their revenge on Vicki and Steven, because she *hadn't* warned them. Never let surface charm fool you – they weren't as decadent as all that, believe me! So it was all very difficult, as you will appreciate.

I couldn't help wishing I hadn't got myself involved in the first place. Zeus knows, it was nothing whatever to do with me; and I must say, the thought of Hesperides grew more attractive by the minute. But it was too late for that now. Here I was, a one-eyed poet, in rough country with lions, no doubt, about – not to mention blood-crazed myth makers – and the only person at all likely to help me was the ineffable Paris, confound him!

Although *why* he should bother, I was unable to say: unless he thought he recognized a kindred spirit, who hated the war as much as he did? Yes, I take the 'confound him!' back. Because, at all events, he had bandaged my face with some sort of soothing herbs he'd found, and been generally pleasant; so I thought I'd better stick with him – at least until I saw my way clear to hopping over the horizon, under my own power.

And what was he on about now? Oh, my name? Yes, of course – and quite reasonable, really. But I've always found it a very good rule to be a bit cautious about handing out the label unless unavoidable – which is why, I'm told, to this day, nobody is entirely convinced that Homer ever existed – so I temporized, as they say. But the only thought which came to me, being rather below par at the time, was what Odysseus had called me, shortly after the operation. So, 'Cyclops,' I said. 'As you observe, one of the Titans.'

Well, he laughed a good deal at that; having had a classical education, and being anxious to prove it, as one always is. 'Oh, that's very good,' he said. 'Cyclops, the one-eyed – couldn't be better! Well, my little Cyclops, my tiny Titan, I think you'd better come back to Troy, and get that wound properly seen to, before you start to fester.'

Just what I wanted, of course; so I went along with that, all right. And then a nerve-scraping thought struck me: 'You don't mean by Cassandra, do you? Because if so, I'd really rather not: I'd sooner just decompose quietly where I am, if it's all the same to you.'

Paris flinched in turn. 'Great Heavens, no! Wouldn't trust her to so much as put a snail on a wart! No – tell you what – that other young sorceress – what's her name? – Cressida, that's it! She'll have you fixed up in no time.'

I couldn't believe my luck – or have agreed more! So off I went, with a comparatively high heart, prepared to give

107

Fate another of my helping hands.

As officer commanding, Paris had no difficulty in getting us down into the labyrinthine catacombs below the city. Not the place I'd have chosen for a convalescent home, left to myself: our guttering, bat-attracting torches, showed only too clearly that several previous patients hadn't come out of it too well. Now they stood skeletally in their recesses, grinning at nothing particularly funny for the rest of eternity: my friend's ancestors, no doubt. Pleased to meet them.

Here and there we passed a guard, who'd been given the crypt concession to serve him right for something or other. And I noticed that, although saluting in a friendly enough way, they *did* seem rather surprised to see us. And then I realized that – of course! – Paris was supposed to be out and about on his Achilles blood-feud business – and *that's* why he was so ready to help me: anything at all to postpone the fatal encounter! So I needn't flatter myself that he enjoyed my conversation or company all that much. Which was something of a relief – because it meant I needn't feel all that indebted to him: and to be going on with, I had quite enough people to try and help out of a mess, without worrying about what was likely to happen to Paris if the Doctor's plan worked. No – he'd just have to take his chance with the rest of them, and the very best of luck!

We eventually found Steven and Vicki in adjacent cells with communicating grating; through which, as we arrived, they were swapping a certain amount of vitriolic back-chat, about whose fault it was they were so situated. Tactless of them, under the circumstances; but fortunately Paris was preoccupied with trying to find the right key, and didn't hear half of it.

'I know quite well how to look after myself,' Vicki was saying, 'there was no need at all for you to come galloping to the rescue! Who do you think you are – the American cavalry?'

I must say, I didn't quite follow that, myself. However, I can only report what I heard.

'All right,' said Steven wearily. 'As long as you're quite sure you've got the message.'

'What message? What are you on about now?'

'I just want you to realize that you've been given exactly one day to find a way of defeating the Greeks.'

'I'm quite aware of that, thank you!'

'Good. And I hope you're also aware that, twenty-four hours ago, the Doctor was given exactly *two* days to find a way of defeating the Trojans. Got that, have you?'

'I'm not a complete fool!'

'Good, again. Because in that case we can leave all the armies and generals and heroes out of the equation, can't we? All we have to remember is that you and the Doctor have got all of today to defeat each other! Happy about it, are you? Confident?'

'Oh, Steven! No – I *hadn't* looked at it quite like that. Me having to beat the Doctor! Golly Moses!'

'That's very quick of you, Cressida,' said Paris, getting the door open at last. 'Yes, I'm afraid you have to be the doctor. I say, you really *can* read the future, can't you? Well done! Yes, I've brought you a patient,' and he ushered me into the cell. 'I'm afraid the poor fellow's had his eye gouged out – so do what you can for him, will you?'

Vicki went pale – because I'm sure I wasn't a sight calculated to amuse and entertain. 'But I don't know anything about –' she was beginning, when I contrived to wink with my remaining eye – not as easy as you might think – and the bright girl took the hint. 'I'll be glad to help if I can,' she said, and fainted. *Very* helpful.

Well, we brought her round without too much trouble; and I was able to take her place on the improvised operating table – a sort of ornamental rack, I think it was.

'Good then,' said Paris, 'I'll leave you to it. If you think he needs an anaesthetic, you can dot him one with that old mace there.' I was rapidly going off him! 'I'll pop in later,

and see how you are. Chin up, Sunshine!' And off he
toddled.

22

Hull Low, Young Lovers

To her evident relief, I dissuaded Vicki from attempting any miracles of modern surgery: so she did a little rudimentary face-mopping and brow-soothing; and, oh yes, she made me a rather sinister eye-patch out of something or other. And then I gave them the glad tidings about the wooden horse. It didn't cheer them up any.

'But when I suggested that to him yesterday,' said Steven – so *he'd* suggested it now? – 'the Doctor said it wouldn't work!'

'Well, now he's been converted,' I said, 'thinks it's the greatest idea since Prometheus invented external combustion! Mind you,' I admitted, 'that's only since he decided man wasn't meant to fly – otherwise we'd have been up to here by now in giant paper darts!'

I explained about that; and, for the first time, Vicki perked up a bit. 'He's gone gaga – thats what it is!' she squeaked. 'If that's his form at the moment, Steven, I'm not so worried about the competition. I'm bound to come up with something at least marginally better than that, I should think.'

'Such as?' he enquired, sourly.

'Well, give me time – I'll get there.'

'As long as you let me know when you have, so that I can work out a way of stopping you. Don't be fatuous, Vicki: if you win, then the Doctor's for the high jump!'

'And if he wins, we are – yes, I keep forgetting. Oh dear, isn't it all complicated?'

'Very,' he gloomed. There was a long silence, to which I contributed as heartily as anyone. I did wonder whether to cheer them up by telling them about Odysseus' plan for do-it-yourself loot, rape, and pillage – but decided against it. No point in piling what'sit on thingummy, is there?

But after a while there was an interruption – provided by young Troilus, in a state of ill-concealed seething jealousy. Well, if it wasn't one prince, it was another.

Steven tactfully removed himself from the grating, where for the last half-hour he'd been doing his impression of 'The Thinker' – and, personally, I pretended to be unconscious. I'd got quite enough to worry about, without getting involved in a teenage tiff!

Before getting down to the main business of the day, Troilus asked who I was.

'Oh, nobody of any importance,' explained Vicki, 'it's just someone who's lost an eye.'

'And you're helping him look for it, I suppose? Really, Cressida – how many men *do* you want in your life?'

She flew at him – as well she might. I wasn't likely contender in 'The most eligible bachelor' stakes, at the time . . . 'I've been nursing him, that's all! I suppose you wouldn't understand about a thing like that, you great musclebound oaf? What do you mean, how many men?'

'Well, what about this Diomede, then? I tell you here and now, I didn't believe a word of that story about meeting him at the Olympic Games. Diana's Grove, indeed! What do you take me for?'

She froze. 'I prefer not to take you at all: but if I have to, it's as a silly little jealous boy, with tantrums! It so happens that Diomede is a very dear friend of mine!'

'A friend? And is that all?'

'All? I suppose you couldn't understand about friendship, would you? Oh no, it's all soppy love and kisses with you, isn't it?'

'As a matter of fact . . .'

'Well, you needn't bother!'

'Very well then, I won't!'

And lots more to the same effect. Really! At a time like this!

'He's in the next cell, I suppose?'

'And what if he is?'

'It just seems very convenient, that's all!'

'Convenient for what?'

'Friendship – so *you* say!'

'Oh, of course it is,' said Vicki. 'The wall's only about three feet thick. Just the thing for playing noughts and crosses on. We do that a lot!'

'I suppose you're going to say now, you don't use the executioner's hatch?'

'The executioner's what? I don't think I know that game.'

'Stop pretending! It's right under your nose, here.' And Troilus swivelled a pivotted stone slab. 'It's the way the headsman comes in at night. If we get a lot of difficult prisoners who look as if they're going to make a fuss, he goes from cell to cell, and kills them while they're asleep. Saves a lot of trouble. I know about it, because father used to send us to play down here, when we were boys. Look, your other friend's got his head on the block now.'

I sat up instantly. Not a pleasant thought.

'Well,' continued Troilus, 'aren't you going to come in, Diomede? I mean, don't let me stop you. I'd hate to think I was in the way . . .'

And so Steven crawled through the hatch, and joined the company – looking rather foolish. Well, I suppose we all did: the opening was obvious enough, now it had been pointed out.

'Only don't try to start anything,' warned Troilus, 'because I've got my sword; and I'm just longing for an excuse to use it!'

You could tell he was: he kept easing the thing in and out of its scabbard. Steven hastened to assure him that he deplored violence in any form – especially that one.

Troilus sneered. 'I suppose that's why Paris was able to capture you? I thought you looked as if there was something lacking!'

Vicki sprang to Steven's defence: 'Look here, Troilus, if you've just dropped in to insult my friend, you can jolly well go back where you came from! I can't think what you're doing here, anyway. I'm sure I don't want to see you.'

'Oh, don't you? Very well – in that case I'll just take your food back to the kitchens.' He picked up a hamper he'd dumped by the door... Our stomachs rumbled as one stomach. He turned in the doorway, and relented. 'Look, are you quite sure you don't want some of this? I've been to an awful lot of trouble to get it – and the others would be furious, if they knew.'

My heart bled for the boy. Love isn't easy at the best of times – and this wasn't one of them.

'Oh, *please*, Troilus,' said Vicki, 'I'm sorry if I was rude – but you were being so silly, and all over nothing. Diomede *is* just my friend, aren't you, Steven?'

'I try to be,' said Steven Diomede, 'but sometimes you make it very difficult.'

'She does, doesn't she?' agreed Troilus. 'I'd noticed that. Well then, everything's all right. I say, do you mind if I join you? I haven't eaten since I got back from patrol.' And he fell upon the salamanders in aspic like a wolf unfolded.

We hastened to compete. At this rate, there wouldn't be a lot left.

'Patrol?' enquired Vicki, between bites, 'Surely you're not mixed up in the fighting, are you? You're too young!'

'These days, military service begins as soon as you can wrestle your weight in wild-cats! Which I can,' he added, unnecessarily. 'Anyway, I'll bet I'm older than you are?'

It was agreed, after some discussion, that they were both eighteen next birthday: and the earth-shattering co-incidence of this, seemed to take their minds off everything else for the time being. They chattered away to each other like a couple of budgerigars who've been at the cuttle-fish a bit. Steven and I looked at each other, and shrugged: youth!

Youth! Quite nauseating!

But at length Steven decided that, although young love might be all very well in its way, it was time to return to the matter in hand.

'I say, Troilus,' he said, 'I'm sorry to interrupt, and all that; but since you two seem to have so much in common, do you think there's any chance you might persuade your father to let us out of here?'

That put a damper on the proceedings, as I could have told him it would. A cloud passed rapidly across the young prince's face and settled in the region of his eye-brows.

'I'm afraid not,' he sighed, 'unless Cressida comes up with a brilliant idea for the war-effort. Don't be misled by those twinkling eyes of his – they're ice-crystals, those are; as most of us have good reason to know. I suppose you *haven't* thought of anything, have you?'

Vicki shook her head, sadly; and I was afraid that under this new-found infatuation of hers, she might be tempted to blow the official secrets act wide open, and tell Troilus what the Doctor was preparing for their entertainment. Love can sometimes play the devil with old loyalties. So I persuaded my mind to race in some last despairing circles and – do you know? it found something, and pounced on it with a glad cry! Of course – there was a way in which Vicki could *seem* to have helped the Trojans, without putting the Doctor at risk. There was one vital little piece of information, which I had forgotten to pass on to them.

'Oh, I don't know, Cressida,' I mused, 'I thought that plan of yours for persuading the whole Greek navy to sail away, was quite brilliant!'

'What plan?' lisped the idiot child.

'Well, obviously, you know far more about it than I do – I'm not entirely sure of the details – but I must say, that spell you concocted put the fear of Olympus into me; and I bet it'll have done the same to the Greeks by now!'

'Oh, *that*?' she said, catching on rather late in the day. 'Do you really think so? It was only an experiment, after all.'

'Well, of course it's only about an hour since you did it, so it may be rather early to say. But it should be dawn by now, and I'd think there'd be some sign of movement, if it's going to work at all. Tell you what, Troilus – why don't you scoot up to one of the watch-towers, and see if the retreat's started yet? I'd be jolly interested to know!'

He looked at me with his eyes popping like seed-pods in summer, so did Vicki and Steven, come to that. Not having my privileged information, they obviously thought my wound had produced new complications of a dangerous nature.

And then Troilus darted off on his errand like Atalanta in a marathon – though remembering, damnit, to lock the cell door behind him. 'Wait here,' he said, ridiculously, 'I'll go and see!'

And off he went.

23

A Victory Celebration

We didn't have to wait very long: he was back in no time, bubbling with euphoria. Yes – the Greeks had gone! Not a ship to be seen anywhere, so presumably they'd sailed for home; and presumably Cressida, the wonder-girl who tells your fortune, speaks your weight, and halves the house-work, was responsible!

Anyway, Paris had gone to make cautiously sure; but there seemed to be no doubt about the matter: and since, as the slogan writers were already saying, a Greek defeat was joy for Troy, would we care to come upstairs to a hastily summoned conference-cum-saturnalia that Priam was preparing for us? Wild revelry, tumult, and little savoury biscuits there would be – he could promise us that!

Well, of course we would so care – although there was some little local difficulty at first about whether Diomede was included in the invitation: I mean 'bring a friend' is one thing, but 'an enemy alien' quite another.

However, as I pointed out, since his former associates and colleagues had left him lurching, there wasn't a lot he could do to undermine Troy all on his own – so why not forget and forgive? And the point was taken – as usual *I* had to think of everything! – so, by the time we entered the State Apartments, we were all congratulating each other like old friends wondering who's going to pay for the drinks! Very uproarious and convivial, the whole thing!

A bevy of dancing girls was high-stepping it about the ballroom, scattering rose petals all over the mosaic – never mind that someone would have to sweep them up afterwards.

Helen was smouldering as usual; but rather thoughtfully, I fancied; because it had probably just occurred to her, amid the general rejoicing, that if Menelaus really had gone back to Sparta, then she could whistle for any alimony she might have been expecting.

And Cassandra, poor dear, had slipped into something more than usually grotesque for the occasion – an eye-catching little snake-skin number, with trimmings of sack-cloth and ashes – because really she'd achieved the necromancer's equivalent of forecasting hail in a heat-wave, hadn't she? But never mind – she'd get her gloomy revenge before too long, if I wasn't very much mistaken . . .

However, old King Priam was on top of his form. He advanced to meet us, dithering with delight, as if to say he'd always known the prodigal daughter would come up trumps; and any fatted calves in the vicinity had better watch out, if they knew what was good for them.

'Cressida, my dear girl,' he said, 'why on earth couldn't you have told us before you were going to do something like this? You'd have saved yourself all that time in the cells – and us a great deal of needless worry!'

'She didn't tell you,' croaked Cassandra, absolutely in mid-season shape, 'because it's some kind of treachery! Don't trust her further, father!'

And she was right, of course. Although the treachery was mine, if anybody's.

'Stuff and silly nonsense!' shouted Priam. 'Go and feed the sacred serpents, or something! If you can't behave pleasantly at a time like this, then I'd rather you didn't infest the festivities at all! Now look – I don't want to be hard on you – why don't you dance with that nice Diomede – he's all on his own? Caper about a bit like the rest of us – enjoy yourself for once – it'll do you good!'

To Steven's wan relief, she didn't seem much taken with the idea, and retired to the outskirts of the proceedings in a marked manner. He beckoned me over to him.

118

'Don't you think, Cyclops, it's time you were on your way?'

This puzzled me. 'I wasn't thinking of going on anywhere just yet,' I said, 'it looks like rather a good party, don't you think?'

'You're not using your head,' he snapped. I liked that! I'd done all the constructive thinking, so far! 'You've got to go and tell the Doctor that we're quite all right now, so he doesn't need to rescue us after all. Tell him to forget about that fool horse, and just meet us at the TARDIS later. Tell him where it is, and suggest we rendezvous there at... say... nine-thirty tomorrow morning. That should give us time to get over the celebrations.'

I couldn't believe my ears! And I was about to explain to him that I didn't think, somehow, it was in the Doctor's gift to cancel the operation, when there was an interruption.

'Ah, here comes Paris,' said Priam, happy to see him for once. 'Well, my boy – have the Greeks really gone?'

'As far as I could tell from a distance,' said Paris, not wishing to commit himself. 'As a matter of fact, I didn't like to go right up to the actual camp-site.'

'Why on earth not? Upon my soul there's nothing to be nervous of now – Achilles will have disappeared with the rest of them! Go back at once, and have a proper look!'

'Well the point is that there *does* seem to be something there; and, I don't really know how to put this, but I *think* it may be the Great Horse of Asia!'

Not the sort of remark, you may think, to contribute much to the party spirit; and, if so, you are right! There was what is known as a rapt silence; and even the hips of the dancing girls bumped and ground to a standstill.

'You think it's *what*?' asked Priam, incredulously.

'Well, if it isn't, it's first cousin to it. Standing all by itself, just this side of the Graecian lines. Look, you should be able to see it from here – it's enormous!'

So the meeting adjourned to one of the watch-towers.

Yes, there it was all right, the Doctor's brain-child – or

mine! And, I must say, even at that distance, it looked formidable – ominous, you know, and somehow sinister. Just a wooden horse, after all . . . but no – there was more to it than that. I tell you, my hackles rose at the sight of it! Odd – very! Even Priam was speechless for once.

Vicki was first off the mark: 'So *that's* the Trojan Horse,' she sighed. 'Oh, dear . . .'

'That's the what, did you say?' asked Troilus.

Cassandra zoomed in, on the instant. 'Yes, ask *her*, you besotted young fool! She knows very well what it is! It is our doom – it is the death of Troy, brought upon us by the cursed witch!'

Paris turned on her: 'Now understand me, Cassandra – I will not have one word said against that horse! It's mine – I found it!'

'And I won't hear one word against Cressida,' said Troilus. 'She's mine – now that I've found her!'

Two brothers, shoulder to shoulder against the world! Jolly impressive – if it hadn't been so tragic.

'Will you not, you pair of degenerate simpletons?' Cassandra said, as if washing her hands of the whole affair. She'd done all she could – and somehow she *knew*, d'you see?

'Then woe to the House of Priam! Woe to the Trojans! And woe to the world, as we've known it!'

Paris looked at her wearily. I think *he* may have known, even then, that she was right – but he'd had enough, and the game was over.

'Well,' he said, 'at any rate, I'm glad you're too late to say "Whoa" to the horse! I've given orders to have it brought into the city!'

24

Doctor in the Horse

'Now once and for all, Steven,' I said, as soon as I couldn't
avoid being alone with him again for a moment, 'nothing
will induce me to go back to that foul Greek camp! Look
what happened to me last time, will you?'

'Please, dear little Cyclops,' put in Vicki, sidling up to
us like the girl of silk and sherbet she'd just discovered she
was. 'If you won't do it for me, think of Helen.'

'I'd rather not, if you don't mind awfully. I've been
trying to keep my attention on other matters ever since I
first saw her.'

'But I know you like her. Surely you don't want her to be
killed, do you?'

I could have spat in her face, if I hadn't been fond of her.
'No red-blooded man is going to kill Helen, you can be
sure of that. But, in any case, I'm not going in reach of
Odysseus again, for you and Helen together in a gift-
wrapped package! I've got my own life to be getting on
with, thank you!'

'Well, that won't take up much of your time in the
future, will it; unless you can manage to stop the Doctor
somehow? You'll be slaughtered with the rest of us,' said
Steven heartlessly. 'So you'd better hurry up, or it will be
too late!'

I saw the point, of course. But why, in Zeus's name, did
it have to be me all the time? I was sick and tired of doing
all the work and getting precious little thanks for it. There
comes a time when a man has got to put his foot down. So

eventually, I put my best one forward, and thinking – damn it! – of Helen all the way, I went back to meet my destiny!

I must say, when I got up close to it, that horse was really something! Those Greeks must have worked – well, like Trojans on a job creation scheme, to get it ready in time!

In fact, I suppose, they must have cobbled it together out of old ships' timbers and drift-wood, and I could see a thigh-bone or two from the old skittle-alley, which had been pressed into service as ribs. But somehow there was more to it than that – as if it had taken on a life of its own; and Odysseus and the Doctor had just fleshed out an idea the gods had thought of anyway. Weird, the whole thing!

But there it stood, nostrils flaring and eyes – Zeus knows what *they* were made of, and *I* don't want to – flashing in the sunset; and you could swear it was almost pawing the ground and panting to be off on its ordained trail to mayhem and murder! And the last of Odysseus' men were just climbing into its sagging belly: so one thing was quite clear – I was too late!

Though what I could have done – what Steven and Vicki could have *expected* me to do – even if I'd got there earlier, I haven't the remotest idea. Once Fate is really on its way with the captions rolling, there's nothing *anyone* can do to stop it, in my experience. Even if I could have contrived to have a quick word with the Doctor, I don't see how that could possibly have helped.

He probably wouldn't have listened to me anyway; and, to be fair there was no earthly reason why he should. 'A man of no importance,' as Vicki so kindly pointed out. But even if he *had* listened, why should Odysseus have paid any attention to *him*? All Odysseus wanted was the sack of Troy, and sharp about it, with drinks on the house afterwards! And the Doctor had shown him how to go about it, and that was the end of his function, thank you – only do try not to get in the way. That's all.

They stood there now, the pair of them, looking up at their creation, as if it were a thing of beauty, and not a horrifying, doom-laden juggernaut.

'Well, Doctor,' Odysseus was saying, as he picked the splinters out of his gnarled hands; 'there's a war-horse and a half for you! That's something like a secret weapon! Better than half-a-dozen of your crack-brained flying-machines!'

The Doctor, to do him justice, was rather more doubtful. 'I wish I shared your confidence,' he said.

'Why, what's the matter? Don't you trust your own invention?'

'It's not that. Oh, the idea's good enough, as ideas go. It's just that the whole contraption looks so mechanically unsound. I mean, just consider those fetlocks: there's no safety margin at all!'

Odysseus gave the offending pastern-joints a cursory glance.

'Well, it hasn't got to last forever, you know. We're not trying to build one of the wonders of the world. As long as it holds together till we're inside Troy, it can collapse into a mare's nest if it wants to.'

'I just wish you understood a few more of the basic principles of mechanics. Supposing we're still inside when it collapses? What then?'

'Then we shall all look extremely silly,' answered Odysseus, philosophically.

'Well, personally I have no wish to be made into a laughing stock! In fact, I've had second thoughts about the whole thing. I think we should cancel the operation while there's still time. I'll find some other way of rescuing my friends.'

'Now, not another word. You've made your horse, and now you must ride in it. Get up that rope-ladder, confound you!' He prodded the Doctor with his cutlass, and together they began the precarious ascent. I tell you, I wouldn't have fancied it. Suddenly the Doctor froze. 'Look out,' he said.

'Oh, what's the matter now? By Zeus, you're making me as nervous as a Bacchante at her first orgy! Get inside, and try to get some sleep!'

'I never felt less like sleep in my life.' I wasn't surprised – they were spinning like spiders in a sand-storm. 'And as to what's the matter, I thought I saw a movement out there on the plain.'

'Well, I should hope you did. That's the whole point of the thing, isn't it? A pretty lot of fools we'd look, if no one took a blind bit of notice of us. So hurry up – and if you find you really can't sleep, I suggest you try counting Trojans. You were quite right, Doctor – here they come now.'

They scambled up the last few rungs of the ladder, and the trap-door closed after them. And that was the last I saw of the Doctor for quite some time.

But I shall always remember how he looked miserably back over his shoulder, that blood-stained evening, so long ago. I think he knew even then, you see, that for once in eternity, all his well-meaning ingenuity had landed him up on the wrong side.

Although, I don't know, perhaps not, after all. Because if the Trojans had won the war, what would have happened to Greek civilization, and all that came later? Would they have been able to produce anything to equal it, I wonder? Impossible to say. It's done – and that's all there is to it.

And the Doctor couldn't have changed things, even if he'd wanted to. And no more could I.

For a fleeting moment, as that company of decent Trojan soldiers marched into the clearing, and took their first awe-struck look at Paris's hellish trophy, the thought crossed my mind that now was the time to say, 'Stop it, you fools! Beware the Greeks bearing gifts!' or words to that effect.

But what would have happened then? First, they'd have destroyed the horse, with the Doctor inside it. And then they'd have gone back home to tell Cassandra she'd been right all the time, before putting Vicki and Steven to death for being involved in the treachery. And I couldn't be a

124

party to all that, could I?

So I let the moment go. There'd been quite enough meddling already. Now I must just let History take its course. And the best I could hope for was to get a good view of it. And considering what was still to happen, *that* was ironic, *if* you like.

25

A Little Touch of Hubris

But as the Trojans began to drag their great, unwieldy prize out of the mud, I realized it was certainly going to take them quite a long time to reach base, to put it mildly – even if it didn't collapse on the way, as seemed likely.

And so after all there *was* just one more thing I could do – I could warn Steven and Vicki to get the TARDIS warmed up while there was still time. So that if and when the Doctor was able to join them, they could zip to infinity without hanging about cranking the starting-handle; or whatever it was they had to do, to get the thing mobile.

I hadn't the remotest idea how it worked, of course – and, what's more, I don't believe they were entirely clear about it, either! Or they wouldn't have kept bouncing about from side to side of N-dimensional space like a snipe on the toot. But that was their business, not mine, Zeus be praised!

In fact, when you thought about it, nobody at this turning point in History appeared to have the vaguest notion about what was going on, or what they should do about it. Perhaps the participants in what later prove to have been great events never do: or is it just that you only need one man with his eye on the ball to urge events onwards? If so, then Odysseus was the fellow in this instance – has to have been!

He had the great advantage, you see, of enjoying violence for its own sake; and that with a pure, clear-sighted unswerving devotion, undistracted by any weak-kneed moral considerations! That's the way to succeed in life, you know: never see anyone's point of view but your own, and you'll romp home past the winning post. Bound to! But it's a difficult trick, and one that I never quite got the hang of.

These Trojans, for instance, obviously had no conception of optimum stress, or moments of inertia; and the horse was straining at every screaming sinew, as they rocked it back and forth, trying to shift it out of the pit its own weight was digging for itself. I imagined that an outbreak of travel-sickness would shortly strike the occupants; so I moved smartly out from under, and retired to a slight distance.

But at last, with a final shuddering groan, the grotesque structure began to move – and once under way, of course, there was no stopping it. Ropes, arms and legs snapped like old bowstrings as it trundled remorselessly forwards.

Funny, what you notice: amidst the general haphazard destruction, one of its vast hooves came down on top of a nest-full of fledgeling larks, which I had been watching with affection. And I remember thinking: 'Yes – and that's only for starters!' Think what Cassandra could have made of an incident like that!

But it was no use hanging about philosophising, so I set off ahead of them towards what I hoped would be my final involvement in this whole misguided farrago.

There was no difficulty about getting in to Troy now: the enormous gates stood wide open, and the whole city seemed to have come out into the streets to enjoy the splendid, triumphal climax of the war. Poor fools! Little did they know that Zeus was about to slip them the staccato tomato!

Before going in, I paused and looked back the way I had come.

Already you could see the approaching monster quite clearly, silhouetted against the full moon; its great, grinning head nodding and tossing, as if to say: 'You wait just a little longer, my dears; and what a nice surprise you're going to have!'

Indescribably ominous and horrible, the whole thing! I shuddered, turned on my heel, and popped back into the palace – while it was still there.

Paris was the hero of the hour – there was no doubt about that. To this day, I cannot imagine why nobody but Cassandra seemed to suspect that anything might be a tiny bit wrong; and that success doesn't come that easily in the affairs of men. Perhaps if Hector had still been alive to lead them, things might have been different.

But again, I don't know: people generally believe what they want to believe – and the Trojans wanted to believe that the war was over at last. And you'll admit they had every excuse for doing so. After all, the Greeks had gone back where they came from, hadn't they? And it seemed they had their new little friend, Cressida, to thank for that.

The general opinion seemed to be that she had somehow conjured this loathsome ancestral god of theirs out of thin air; and it was this macabre manifestation which had finally persuaded the superstitious, Olympus-orientated Greeks that the game was up. So the least the Trojans could do under the circumstances was to invite the faithful old horse in for a bundle of hay and a bit of a sing-song. Churlish not to, in fact. Quite.

So there Vicki was; guest of honour at the victory banquet – and how she was ever going to find an excuse for slipping away to the TARDIS for a moment, I couldn't imagine. Not that she showed any sign of wanting to. The silly, infatuated child was so enraptured with young Troilus, that I honestly believe that during my absence, she'd contrived to forget the ghastly danger they were in. Women!

Even Steven appeared to be having the time of his life: because the real Diomede had been quite a fellow, it seemed. Not perhaps in the very first rank of heroes, like Ajax and Achilles; but still a likely contender for second place in the hierarchy. And now that the war was over, and he'd been captured, they couldn't wait to say what a splendid chap they'd always thought him – our very gallant enemy, and so forth. I'll swear, they were even arranging to hold anniversary reunions, when the veterans could all swap reminiscences, and get drunk together!

Well, I hated to drag them both away to disillusion, but the job had to be done somehow – only the trouble was, they were so busy being lionised, I couldn't see how I was going to get near them.

And then, amidst the general brouha-ha and rejoicing, I noticed a rather striking looking girl called Katarina, who was crying conspicuously to herself in a corner, and looking rather left out of things. I'd had occasion to notice her before: one of Cassandra's accolytes, she seemed to be, and although that certainly wasn't a job calculated to cheer anyone up a great deal, nevertheless I thought she was rather overdoing the soul-sick lamentation business. So I buck and winged my way over to her through the merry throng, and, sensing a possible ally, asked her what was the matter.

She took one look at me, and screamed. I kept forgetting that, since my injury, mine wasn't the sort of face you'd be happy to use as a model for the bedroom frescos – but I managed to calm her down eventually.

Whereupon she gave me some rigmarole about one of the sacred doves, for which she was responsible, having died, regretted by all; and that the subsequent post-mortem had revealed its liver was all to blazes. Which meant, apparently, that doom and disaster must surely follow – particularly when Cassandra got to hear about it: and not only a general cataclysm would there be, but a more personalized version, closely involving herself and Nemesis.

Well, I couldn't give her an argument about the first; because round about now the cheers of the populace out in the square reached a crescendo, and a quick glance through the window revealed that super-horse was negotiating the home straight. But as to the second, it

seemed to me that her extremity might be my opportunity
– for getting both her and Vicki out of harm's way, that is.
For I knew my young friend fairly well by now: and
whereas she wasn't likely to leave Troilus for the purpose
of saving her own skin – lovers frown on that sort of thing,
for some reason – she might very well do so to save
someone else's. Or so I reasoned.

So, 'Listen, pretty child,' I said to Katarina, 'your uncle
Cyclops has the cure for what ails you! Or rather, Cressida
has; being altogether more of a force to be reckoned with
than your superior as events have shown. So go and tell her
from me, that if she'll take you at once to that portable
temple of hers, she'll find the necessary on the bottom shelf
of the altar; filed under antidotes, panaceas, and elixirs,
doom-struck for the use of. Say that the Doctor will be
there in no time, and then everything will be roses and
ambrosia for both of you. If she gives you an argument, tell
her it's a special favour to me, in return for past services.'

Well, she looked rather surprised – as well she might –
but sensible girls don't argue with men who look like I did
at the time; and off she went – to find a happy deliverance,
or so I sincerely hoped.

At any rate, I could hardly do more in that direction; and
so I made a circuitous way towards Steven, the well-known
and popular Diomede, who was attempting a trick with
two chairs, to general acclamation; and I gambled on the
possibility that he would shortly appeal for an assistant.
Because I knew the trick, but did he? I doubted it.

And it also occured to me that I really ought to have a
shot at removing Troilus, at least, from the disaster area;
and I'd thought of a plan. Oh, ingenuity was positively
bursting out of my ears, that Apocalyptic evening!

26

Abandon Ship!

I'd told Katarina to pile on the agony a bit; because it was going to take more than a sick headache to prize Vicki away from the proceedings – I could tell that. So I watched with some concern as she listened to the tale of woe; and such an interesting blend of expressions flitted anxiously about her face that it fairly broke my heart to see it.

Her first reaction, of course, was to consult Troilus in the matter: but fortunately he'd chosen that moment to step out onto the balcony with Paris and their father, to acknowledge the vox of the populi.

Then the poor tortured child, so happy a moment ago, but now torn by divided loyalties, seemed to come to a decision – and not before time! She looked across the crowded room, that disenchanted evening, and caught my remaining eye; then she nodded gloomily, gave me a pathetic wave, brushed away a tear or two – and, having dealt with these formalities, slipped silently out into the night with Katarina. Well done, that girl!

Relieved, I turned to the next item on my agenda, and tapped Steven on the shoulder – by bad luck choosing rather a crucial moment in his routine, and causing him to drop one of the chairs on his toe.

'What in Hades are you doing back here?' he snarled, in welcome.

'I was too late,' I told him. 'And if you'll stop showing off for a moment, and give your attention to the speciality act at the top of the bill, you'll see that the horse is waiting in the wings with fun and massacre for all, regardless of expense. Vicki has therefore gone to wait for the Doctor in the TARDIS. Go and do thou likewise!'

To do him credit, he got my drift at once; and pausing only to say he thought it a bit thick that I hadn't managed to hold up the invading force on my own, he handed me his remaining chair, and set off after the others.

So that was that. Except for Troilus, of course.

I had toyed with the idea of sending him to the TARDIS as well, so that he could live happily ever after with Vicki; but on second thoughts, I realized that wouldn't do at all. Apart from my not knowing how many passengers the thing was licensed for, I wasn't, on reflection, at all sure how he would react. Even though he was in love with his Cressida, he was still a loyal Trojan – and might even decide to arrest the whole boiling of them, when he discovered what he would take to be their treachery.

That's the trouble with these clean-limbed, clear-eyed types, with determined jaws: they're liable to put Country before Love, and Honour before either of them, if you catch them in the wrong mood. So you have to be a bit careful and sound the ground.

Another thing was that the Doctor was unlikely to find a chance of making his excuses to his new cronies, and sprinting for the TARDIS, until after the battle had commenced, and they were busy with other matters; so it was going to be a close-run thing anyway, without his having jealous young princes arguing the toss about the rights and wrongs of the proceedings.

No – I did what I hoped was the next best thing – and never mind having to live with myself afterwards; I'd got used to that over the years, and you can't always choose the company you'd like.

'Dear young Prince of the blood,' I said; 'am I right in supposing that my friend Cressida is dearer to you than all the jewels of the Orient, and sweeter than Springtime, to boot?'

He thought for a moment. 'I wouldn't have put it quite

like that myself,' he mused, 'but the supposition is sound in essentials.'

'Then,' I said, treacherously, but meaning well, 'I think you should know that she and Diomede have just strolled outside for a moment. They spoke of a short walk in the moonlight – out in the countryside . . .'

He sagged at the knees, as well he might, poor boy. 'Thank you, Cyclops,' he said, 'I shan't forget this.' I knew *I* wouldn't, either; *or* forgive myself, come to that. But it was in a good cause.

I watched him from the balcony, as he elbowed his way through the crowd in the square; then, once clear, he sprinted like a cheetah who's just remembered an appointment, out through the gates, and into the darkness of the plain – where, Zeus willing, he would be safe from the wrath to come. And – who knows? – it was even possible that Vicki might get to hear about it one day, wherever she was going; and perhaps she might thank me.

Well, I could do no more. I looked round at all the happy, pleasant, and – yes – civilized people I had learnt to be fond of but, of course, there was no way of saving them. In fact, I had probably interfered too much already.

Paris was a charming, intelligent man; but he really *did* deserve what was coming to him – as don't we all, when you think about it? Priam was a fairly benevolent old despot, but he'd perpetrated an outrage or two in his time – *must* have done, to get where he was! And although even Cassandra probably had a point or so in her favour if you looked closely – never mind, she was about to be proved right about most things, which is more comfort that most of us get, in the end.

And, Hades, nobody lives forever, do they? I mean, what do you want – miracles?

So I didn't say 'goodbye' to anyone – but, rather sadly, made my way out into the square. Did I only fancy I saw the Doctor's wise and worried old face, looking out from one of the horse's eye-holes as I passed? '*Is* there a doctor in the horse?' I wondered, without much humour. Well, I couldn't be sure – but I waved anyway. And then I wandered slowly out through the gates, and turned my back on Troy for the last time.

Or rather, such had been my intention; but a couple of leagues from the doomed walls, I thought I might as well see the end of the affair from a safe distance – so I sat down on a hillock in the moonlight, and awaited developments. After all, if you remember, that's what I'd come for. I was a writer – and it would all make good copy one day, wouldn't it?

And so that was the last of the mistakes I was to make in this whole sorry saga. Because I'd forgotten about Achilles, hadn't I?

The scruff of my neck was seized in what is known as a vice-like grip; and I was flung, struggling and spitting like a kitten, into the heart of a gorse-bush.

'Well, little Cyclops,' he enquired, 'whose side are you on *this* time?'

And, under all the circumstances, I found it very difficult to say.

27

Armageddon and After

Achilles wasn't in the best of moods anyway – you could
see that. No doubt he felt he'd been passed over in favour of
an older man; and furthermore, an older man he heartily
disliked. Why, he wondered, should Odysseus get all the
glory; while he, Achilles, the best damn' warrior in the
regiment, had to skulk about away from the action, in
charge of the reinforcements? So he took it out on me.

'We quite thought you were dead, you know,' he
remarked pleasantly. 'Odysseus thought he'd killed you
the other evening: then apparently your body disappeared,
and he began to wonder. That's the trouble with Odysseus;
the poor old boy gets delusions – half the time he doesn't
know his breakfast from Wednesday! Well, as usual, I
suppose I shall have to finish the job off properly for him.
We don't want to leave any loose ends, do we?'

He didn't bother with blank verse for me, you notice?
Oh no – they save that sort of courtesy for each other. A
class thing really, I take it. But it's the sort of slight which
hurts.

'Now then,' he continued, 'any last requests, before I see
the colour of your tripes?'

I couldn't think of any; and after waiting patiently for a
bored second or so, he drew his sword. 'Well then, we'd
better get on with it. No point in hanging about, is there,
when a thing's got to be done?'

The blade glinted in the moonlight – Damascus steel, I
noticed; very smart! – as he raised his arm for the thrust. I

135

mean, you don't expect steel in the bronze age, do you? And I would like to say that my whole past flashed before me – but it didn't. In fact, I wouldn't let it – I wanted no part of my past, since it had brought me to this! No, I just had time to think that, after all, I'd be seeing Priam and the boys in Hades any moment now, when there came one of those unexpected interruptions, the gods are fortunately so good at.

'Diomede!' called Troilus, approaching at a gallop. 'You and I are going to settle this Cressida business, once and for all!'

With a muttered apology to me for the delay, Achilles turned to face him, smiling like a scimitar. 'Wrong hero, I'm afraid, my little cadet! Diomede is dead – so perhaps Achilles can oblige you?'

For a moment Troilus looked a bit like a very young terrier who's stumbled on a tiger, sleeping it off in a fox-hole. But only for a moment. He was made of good stuff, that boy!

'My brother Hector's murderer? Well, it seems you feared to face Paris' – loyal to the last, you see? – 'but I thank Zeus for setting you before me! Now, go to seek your friend Patroclus . . .' And he flew at the sneering muscle-man like a falcon on a good day.

Well, a falcon he may have been – but Achilles was an eagle, make no mistake about that! And it seemed to me there could be only one end to this ill-advised encounter, as they whirled and pirouetted about the plain, swapping insults and carving the occasional slice out of each other. Troilus was game, all right, but he wasn't an Odysseus by any means, and that was the sort of solid oak article the situation called for. He was also inexperienced at this sort of thing, while Achilles was the best the Greeks had to offer. Even Hector hadn't found him a walk-over, if you remember? No – I had grown fond of Troilus, and I didn't think I could bear to watch.

And pretty soon I couldn't anyway – because a back-hand swipe by Achilles caught me across what was left of my ruined face. And that was the end of my surviving eye!

I was thinking as I lay there, bleeding in the dust, that, while wishing Troilus all the luck in the world, I would rather Achilles finished him off as quickly as convenient; so that he could turn his attention to me, and end the matter as promised. Life had not had my best interests at heart for some time, I considered; and the sooner I was out of it, the better.

One does think like that, at times. A passing mood, of course.

And before long I heard what could only be a death-cry – a thoroughly unpleasant gargling noise; then the crashing collapse of an armoured body, sounding like a felled tree, screaming to ruin in the sudden silence; and I braced myself for my coming quietus.

'Come on, little Cyclops,' said my friend Troilus. 'You can get up now – it's all over!' And he took my shattered head in his arms, bless him!

'Forgive me, Troilus,' I said, once I could speak again, 'but what happened? Please don't think I haven't every confidence in you, but how in Hades did you bring *that* off?'

'Achilles caught his heel in the brambles – stumbled, and that was it. I had him.' His heel? Wouldn't you know? Those oracles can tell us a thing or two, can't they, if we'll only listen!

'And now,' said Troilus, 'let me help you back home, where you can be looked after properly.'

Well, of course, *that* was the last thing I wanted; and I was about to explain that current medical thinking would incline to the suggestion that I rest where I damn' well was for a bit, when the most appalling racket I ever heard erupted in the far distance, as Odysseus and his men started operations.

And soon there was no place like home – or nothing to speak of, anyway. Armageddon just wasn't it in, for nations furiously raging!

And so we sat there, the two of us, alone in the darkness;

while Troy, and all the sane sophistication it stood for, disappeared amongst what are laughingly called the myths of antiquity.

Ironic, isn't it? Your man in Scamander, with the greatest scoop of his life being enacted before him, unable to see a blind – forgive me – thing!

So I'm afraid I can't tell you very much about it, after all. But as far as ear-witnessing is concerned, I could do that all right – and soon began to wish I couldn't: the roar and crackle of flames, the crash of masonry as the topless towers tumbled to rubble, and the bubbling sobs of the slaughtered.

And then, *above* all that, if you'll believe me, there rose that extraordinary noise I'd heard once before – could it only have been three days ago? – when the TARDIS first appeared on the sun-baked plain; and the great Hector, finest warrior of them all, met his undignified end as a consequence.

So I knew that my pathetic little plans had worked; and out of all the chaos at least the Doctor and his friends were away and clear – off to their next appointment in the Fourth Dimension, if that's what it's called. And I was glad; becaue I'd grown fond of them all – especially little love-lorn Vicki!

And so I explained to Troilus about the TARDIS; and about how I had deceived him, but only to save his life; and how his Cressida had loved him – but that it wouldn't have worked in the long-run, because time-travellers are really a different class of person, and you never know where to look for them next.

Then suddenly he sat up, and stopped crying for everything he'd lost; and I thought, 'Right! So this is where I get it in the thorax – and about time, too, after the mess I've made of things!'

And then I heard, close at hand, the sound of something he'd already seen – light footsteps pattering towards us across the plain; and the next minute Vicki – his little Cressida – rushed into his arms with what is usually described as a whoop of joy!

And after that, I couldn't get much sense out of either of them for quite a while.

Well, of course, as I might have guessed if I'd had time to think about it, she had very sensibly decided to let Katarina go adventuring with the Doctor and Steven in her place; and to settle down where her heart was. Because you've got to make up your mind where you really belong sometime, haven't you? And the sooner the better, once you've fallen in love. A splendid outcome, I call it. The only problem being that they couldn't belong to Troy, because it wasn't there!

So for three days we stayed starving in our hide-away, while the vultures circled in the packed rapacious sky, and the smoke rose from the ruins. And they told me how Odysseus – who was now half-convinced that the Doctor *was* Zeus by the way! – and Agamemnon and the rest of the surviving heroes carried their booty of art treasures back to the galleys; one day to form the nucleus of the Parthenon collection, no doubt. And how Menelaus and Helen – so she *was* all right: good! – gesticulated angrily at each other all the way down to the beach. And then, how they all sailed away for home. And so the story was over at last. And where did that leave *us*, you may ask?

Well, soon after the Greeks had gone, we saw horsemen approaching: and, heaven be praised, it was Aeneas and the Trojan cavalry, come back too late to do anything but save our skins for us.

And as Aeneas readily agreed, there seemed little to detain us: so we set off together to found a new Troy elsewhere. And we thought of calling it Rome.

Only *we* looked in at Carthage on the way, and one thing led to another, as usual – and that will be several more stories I must write one day, when I've time.

Yes, Troilus and Cressida have looked after their blind friend very well, over the years. I suppose they felt that they owed me something – which makes a pleasant change!

And I haven't been idle: my great epic about the Trojan War has sold extremely well. But if you ever read *The Iliad* – snappy title, don't you think? – you mustn't be surprised if you find no mention in it of the Doctor and the TARDIS.

No, I've put all that side of things down to Zeus and the Olympians.

Because that's what the public expects – and you have to give them *that*, don't you? But just once, before I die, I thought I'd like to come back here and remember what *really* happened ... and tell it like it was ...

And so, that's what I've done.

Epilogue

After the old blind poet had finished speaking, there was silence in the olive-grove for a while. Well, silence except for the cicadas; and a steady munching noise as his audience of one finished off the last of the goat-cheese.

Having done so, he cleared his throat, and clambered rather laboriously to his feet: because he was an old man, too; although not so old as Homer.

'Yes,' he said, 'I must say I was glad to get out of that horse. The nastiest contraption I've ever had the misfortune to travel in – and *that's* saying something!'

The poet smiled, and turned his sightless eyes towards him. 'So it *is* you? I thought so. I've always known! Once in the market place at Alexandria, you caught my arm, and led me off before the mob burned the library.'

'So I should hope! A distinguished author, like you.'

'And another time, in Carthage – you saved Aeneas, didn't you?'

'He needed saving! He'd wasted far too much time with that woman – and he had a city to build. Well, I'm glad to find you so well. And tell me: how is Vicki?'

'Middle-aged, I'm afraid.'

'Ah yes, I suppose she would be by now. Should have stayed with me, you know – then she'd still have been eighteen!'

'But not in love.'

'Great Heavens, is she still? You do surprise me! Well, give her my regards, won't you?' And the Doctor brushed the crumbs off his frock-coat, and stumped away to try and remember where he'd parked the TARDIS.